COVERT GAMES

REDEMPTION HARBOR SERIES

Katie Reus

Cover art: Jaycee of Sweet 'N Spicy Designs
Editors: Kelli Collins & Julia Ganis
Author website: http://www.katiereus.com

Covert Games /Katie Reus. -- 1st ed.
KR Press, LLC

ISBN-13: 9781635560558
ISBN-10: 1-63556-055-1

eISBN: 9781635560541

For Kari. Thank you again for our caffeine fueled (on my part) writer's getaway and helping plot out this book. You are the best in so many ways.

Praise for the novels of Katie Reus

"Exciting in more ways than one, well-paced and smoothly written, I'd recommend *A Covert Affair* to any romantic suspense reader."
—Harlequin Junkie

"Sexy military romantic suspense." —USA Today

"I could not put this book down. . . . Let me be clear that I am not saying that this was a good book *for* a paranormal genre; it was an excellent romance read, *period*." —All About Romance

"Reus strikes just the right balance of steamy sexual tension and nail-biting action....This romantic thriller reliably hits every note that fans of the genre will expect." —*Publishers Weekly*

"Prepare yourself for the start of a great new series! . . . I'm excited about reading more about this great group of characters."
—Fresh Fiction

"Wow! This powerful, passionate hero sizzles with sheer deliciousness. I loved every sexy twist of this fun & exhilarating tale. Katie Reus delivers!" —Carolyn Crane, RITA award winning author

"A sexy, well-crafted paranormal romance that succeeds with smart characters and creative world building."—Kirkus Reviews

"*Mating Instinct*'s romance is taut and passionate . . . Katie Reus's newest installment in her Moon Shifter series will leave readers breathless!"
—Stephanie Tyler, *New York Times* bestselling author

CHAPTER ONE

—It's always a good time to do the right thing.—

"Hey, thanks for seeing me," Hazel said to Leighton as she stepped into the lobby of Redemption Harbor Consulting. Instead of her normal FBI "uniform" of a pantsuit, today she wore jeans, a sweater and sneakers.

"Of course." Leighton nodded as he moved to lock the front door. No one else was at the office this late.

Hell, no one except a select few even knew this building existed. Gage, hacker extraordinaire, had worked his magic, and while they paid taxes on the building, this particular warehouse was listed as something else entirely. Redemption Harbor Consulting was a building on the other side of town. It had desks and offices and everything one would expect from a consulting company. But they didn't actually do any work there. Instead, they had it rigged with security cameras, and monitored it remotely. It was their front in case they ever needed it.

But FBI Special Agent Hazel Blake wasn't just anyone. She was a federal agent who had done them more than one favor. Of course, they'd done favors for her as well.

More than that, she was Leighton's friend. They'd been overseas at the same time together on occasion and, other than his crew here, she was one of the few people he truly loved and trusted with his life.

"You sounded urgent," he said referring to her text. "What's up?" Since she was a Fed, it seemed strange she'd be here asking them for help with a job, but maybe she needed to go off the books for something.

Expression tense, she pulled a manila folder out of a purse the size of a backpack. She'd cut her jet-black hair since the last time he'd seen her. It was now in a sharp bob around her face. "We can do this in one of the conference rooms or right here."

"Conference room is fine. No one else is here tonight. Is this a case you want us to take on?" he asked as they headed down the nearest hallway.

Recently Skye, one of the cofounders, had added a giant oil painting of a crab tap dancing to one of the walls. He had no idea why but it made him smile every time he passed it. Hell, maybe that was the why. For all her tough exterior, Skye loved this crew.

"Nice," Hazel said, snorting softly as they walked by it.

"Skye."

"Ah."

In other words, no explanation necessary.

"This is all off the books," Hazel said as they sat at one end of the long conference table.

He gave her a dry look.

"I know, I know. Everything you do is off the books. I just want that clear up front so there's no misunderstanding. This is personal for me. It has nothing to do with the Bureau. Not really anyway."

"All right," he said.

Sighing, she flipped open the folder. "All the details are here. But basically, my grandmother's neighbor got into debt with the wrong person. A loan shark who works for Alexei Kuznetsov."

Okay, now she had Leighton's attention. "I thought you guys were building a case against him." She'd never actually said the FBI was, but she'd hinted at it once over beers a few weeks ago.

She lifted a shoulder, not confirming one way or another. "You know I can't talk about that. But...hypothetically, say we are building a case against him. That would be another reason I can't get involved with this. I hate to say it, but this thing I'm giving you is too small for my people. I have to look at the bigger picture. We need to bring down the entire operation. Cut off the head of the snake. Not take down a small portion of his operation. Because this would do nothing, and he'll just keep going and keep hurting people." She motioned to the file even though he wasn't sure what was in it yet.

Leighton thought he knew what she was trying to say. Because on an intellectual level, he understood the greater good. Even if he sometimes morally struggled with it, he absolutely understood that sometimes the needs of the majority counted more than a few small fish. It was just very hard to digest when you were staring directly at one of the "small fish" right in front of you and unable to save their life.

He closed his eyes once and a long-ago image flashed in his mind. A photograph of a charred teddy bear with one eye and a missing foot.

Nope.

He opened his eyes, shoving that image right back where it belonged. Far away from the present. "We've been building a file on him," Leighton said. It was a secret but not one he needed to keep from Hazel. Hell, she must know they were. Kuznetsov was on their radar now.

"I hoped you guys were. It also goes without saying, you guys better stay off the Bureau's radar."

"Come on." They knew how to be ghosts, how to be invisible. Two of their crew, Skye and Colt, had been actual spies. And Savage had been pretty damn close to being one, with all the covert work he'd done.

"So my grandma's neighbor got in deep with this bookie. To pay off the debt," she shook her head, her jaw tightening as she seemed to collect herself, "the bookie made an offer. This family would lose everything and he would kill the father—Rico, the loser who got them into debt in the first place—or one of Rico's daughters could work off the debt on her back."

Leighton balled his hands into fists. "How old is this girl?"

"In her twenties. Of age. Doesn't make it any better."

Hazel moved one of the papers out of the way and Leighton got a good look at the girl. Her name was Maria Lopez. She was young, college-aged, with long brown hair, pretty brown eyes, a nice smile. *Hell.* "So what do you need me to do?"

"This guy, Marco Broussard, is part of Kuznetsov's organization. He and his crew run women out of three of his hotels—allegedly. They're all in New Orleans. One's a hotel and casino. I don't know where she is exactly, but I promised my grandmother I would bring the girl home. The mom found out about the situation too late. She's already left her piece-of-shit husband and is desperate to get her oldest daughter back. But she can't find her and has no one to turn to."

"You've got to have an idea where she's being held if you know he runs women out of three hotels. You guys seriously can't go after her?"

"We could, but it would tip Kuznetsov off that we're on to him. The Feds aren't going to stick their neck out over one girl. Or even a bunch of girls. And he knows that. So he'd know we were looking at him. He could shut down all of his New Orleans operations. And we're already working other angles there—we're so close to bringing him down."

Leighton frowned, understanding but not liking it. It was why he could never work for the government. Never again. "How did the family even know to come to you?"

"The neighbor saw a picture of me in my Air Force uniform on my grandmother's mantel. She's got my military picture and a picture of me the day I graduated from Quantico."

Leighton nodded. "Okay. So you want us to extract the girl and then what?"

"If you get her out, I'm going to get the girl and her mother somewhere safe. I don't give a shit what happens to Rico. That sorry excuse for a human basically pimped out his own daughter, making her feel guilty enough that she left of her own volition when her mother was out of the house. He can rot in hell."

Leighton nodded again. "What about the rest of Kuznetsov's operation?"

"We're working to bring it all down. Before that happens, I need to do this for my grandmother. For this girl. I can't save everyone, but if I can just save one..." She shook her head. "Jesus, I just need to do this."

Leighton understood what she wasn't saying, could read it in her expression and hear it in her tone. There was so much shit in the world every day it was like an avalanche of garbage that they were all drowning in. She wanted to do this one thing to help balance the scales, and he would definitely help her. "If I can get more girls out, I'm going to. I'll go after this one for you. But I know my crew. You do too. If we can help more than just her, we're sure as hell going to. We're not gonna stop at one."

Hazel gave him a small grin as if she'd expected that. "Why do you think I came to you? I'm focused on what I need to be focused on. But since you said that..." She pulled out another piece of paper and laid it on top of the stack. "This should be interesting to you. And you better burn this shit once you memorize it."

His eyes widened slightly as he scanned the details. As soon as she was gone, he needed to contact the rest of the crew.

It was time for a company meeting.

He straightened the papers and shut the little manila folder before looking back up at Hazel. "You're out late tonight."

"Yeah," she said. "And headed home after this. Melissa said she'd have dinner waiting." Hazel shook her head once. "I seriously don't know what I did to deserve her."

He nearly laughed. Hazel was one of the most giving people he'd ever known. She deserved happiness if anyone did. "You guys set a date yet?"

His friend grinned. "Yeah. If it was up to me we'd just do a courthouse wedding."

"Tell me you didn't suggest that."

Hazel winced slightly. "Maybe."

He laughed, shaking his head. "Damn, woman. Even I know that's not cool."

Hazel lifted a shoulder. "Well, now I know too. Melissa looked at me like I'd said we should sacrifice kittens, so I figured we better do this right. And you're definitely going to be my best man."

"Sounds good," he said, standing. "Get home to your fiancée. I'm going to call a meeting with everybody tomorrow. I'll keep you updated when possible."

"Thank you for this." She pulled him into a tight hug before stepping back. "I know the way out. Talk to you soon."

* * *

Leighton sat with the others the next morning as Gage worked his magic on his computer, his fingers moving at warp speed. Everyone had arrived this morning ready to go over the file Hazel had given him. Thankfully, Skye had brought a box of pastries—though she'd eaten half of them herself already.

"Okay, so I took what Hazel gave us," Gage said, leaning forward slightly in his chair as he pulled up a document on one of his many oversized screens. "I've got the schematics of each hotel and I managed to hack into two of their security systems using weaknesses. I don't have full access, but I've got enough right now that I'm piggybacked onto their exterior cameras and some of their interior ones. But...I couldn't get into this one. The Sapphire. The one Kuznetsov's niece manages."

"Why not this one?" Leighton asked. According to the files, they were all in New Orleans and fairly close to one another. One was in the business district and two were in the French Quarter.

"I hacked the others using unpatched—and potentially unknown—vulnerabilities. One using an old webcam, and the other..." He trailed off, frowning as he appeared to hit another wall. "I don't want to say this place is unhackable, but I need to be inside it to see if I can find any weak spots. This one is a casino as well as a hotel, while the first two are just hotels. The security is tighter here. And given how tight it is, if I go in there and get tagged by a security camera—if he knows who I am—there's a good chance it will negate the peace between Brooks and Kuznetsov," Gage added, saying what they all knew.

They'd gotten tangled up with Alexei Kuznetsov on a previous job. More specifically, Brooks had. It was very likely that the criminal didn't know exactly what Redemption Harbor Consulting truly did or how much they'd been digging up on him. But it also stood to reason that if Brooks was keeping tabs on Kuznetsov, the other man was doing the same, and he might know more about their crew than they wanted. So they had to be smart about how they went after him. Kuznetsov knew Brooks had blackmail material on the guy's son, and that Brooks knew about the existence of a daughter he'd worked very hard to keep secret from most people.

Despite all that, clearly someone needed to be inside The Sapphire. If that woman was being trafficked through one of Kuznetsov's places, they needed to know where. Either through hacking the camera systems or with eyes on the ground.

"I'll be the one who goes into his hotel," Leighton said, looking at the rest of the crew: Skye, Colt, Savage, Olivia, Brooks and Nova. Darcy might be married to Brooks, but she had her own business to run and wasn't here for this.

"Nah, we can figure it out later," Colt said, shaking his head. "You don't have to take this on."

"I've been out of town for the last few jobs. Hell, most of my jobs have been far away from the South. And...I'm the only one without a significant other. I know we're all capable, but this shit is going to be dangerous if Kuznetsov figures out what I'm up to." For some reason, his friends seemed to think he was fragile lately. Maybe not lately, even. He'd been withdrawn since making the move to civilian life—as civilian as this would ever be—but he could handle his business.

"If he does, we'll all be targets regardless." Skye's tone was neutral.

"I know, but I still think I should be the one to go in. I don't have anyone to worry about back home. Or to worry about me." Which meant he'd be completely free of all the baggage that could wear on someone while on a job. "And if we need to target his niece for information..." He trailed off, not needing to finish the thought. They weren't in the business of using sex to gain information. Ever. But he was single and none of the other guys were. That little fact mattered, since Kuznetsov's niece basically ran the hotel and casino. And Hazel had come to him with this. He wanted to be the one leading this op. Hell, he needed to—maybe it would cleanse his soul. Or at least even the karmic scale a little.

"I'm with Leighton on this," Gage said, right before he grinned like an evil cartoon villain—which was usually how he acted when he'd already come up with a plan on his own. "I knew we'd be infiltrating this place so I've already created a persona for you," he continued. "Actually, it's one of the cover IDs I've been working on for a while, so it's solid and established—and you're going to take it over. Your name is Spencer Johnson. You're a big baller who doesn't mind throwing around his money. You're a trust fund jackass who's not quite like the normal trust fund crowd. You've started some businesses of your own that are successful and you've gotten into real estate development on the periphery. A silent investor of sorts on some projects. You like to have a good time, you're not flashy, and you don't dress too extravagantly. And you don't have many vices...except prostitutes. High-dollar escorts, to be specific. That and occasionally gambling. Blackjack mainly. Since this is your first time in New Orleans, you're going to want to enjoy yourself."

"Classy," Nova muttered.

"Anyway," Gage continued after grinning at his fiancée, "Once you're inside, I can do the rest remotely and see if I can hack into their system. After that happens, I should be able to get eyes everywhere and see if we can spot the girl. Obviously I haven't seen her at the other two hotels or this would all be a moot point. But that doesn't mean she's not there either, so I'll be monitoring the cameras with facial recognition software. More than anything, we need feet and eyes on the ground in New Orleans."

A new picture appeared on screen, this time of a beautiful woman in her twenties. Luciana Carreras. Kuznetsov's niece. His dead brother's daughter. For some reason, she didn't have the same last name as her uncle, but had taken her mother's maiden name instead. Long dark hair, pouty lips, petite and curvy. Leighton recognized the woman from the file Hazel had given him. She was stunning, and he didn't give a fuck. Because she was related to a monster and okay with running the very business that might sell women into sex slavery.

"A beautiful monster," he muttered.

Gage turned around in his chair, frowned. "We don't know that she's involved yet." He turned back and started clicking away on his keyboard. "In fact, her financials indicate that she lives a pretty normal life. Well, normal-ish. When her parents died, her uncle was in charge of her trust. He's used some of it for her schooling, but mainly he's paid for her college and other expenses directly. Her trust is basically untouched, and she started working for him as soon as she graduated—even though she had a lot of offers on the table. Better offers. If I had to guess, she might've taken the job because they're related. Not that it matters. But from the surface, she looks clean. Her only crime is being related to the man. Most of his businesses are directly on the East Coast, with a few exceptions—the three hotels in New Orleans being some of those exceptions. With what Hazel has told us and the Feds' presence there now, it's likely because he's starting to run shit through the Gulf Coast."

Leighton grunted once. "She could have taken his job offer because they're making money off the pain of others."

Gage lifted one shoulder. "Maybe. If so, we'll bring her down too. But...just let me keep looking. I've found some interesting things about her."

"Interesting how?" Skye asked, straightening slightly next to Colt. It was a miracle she was sitting still at all. Normally she was pacing.

Gage's shoulders stiffened ever so slightly, as they always did when someone tried to rush him. He claimed that his genius couldn't be rushed. "I'll let you know what

I find when I find it. For now, I've got everything we need to stealthily infiltrate the hotel and casino."

"All right. So what else have you got for us?" Skye asked.

"*Patience.* I'm not your dancing monkey," Gage muttered, his lips twitching.

"Exactly. Dancing monkeys listen better."

Gage laughed lightly as he pulled up another screen. "That extra intel Hazel gave us was spot on."

Leighton looked at the rows of information scrolling across the screen. "That bastard really has his dirty fingers in everything, doesn't he," Leighton muttered. The list was written in a sort of code, but some of the codes were clear enough that one of Kuznetsov's front businesses was smuggling people and weapons.

"Vienna already got back to me," Skye said, referring to a smuggler she and Colt had worked with in the past.

Leighton had met the woman before and she was all right. Her job was unconventional, aka shady as fuck, but who was he to judge? Because she sure as hell wasn't smuggling people or anything that could hurt others. "Already?"

"Yep," Skye said. "She hates Kuznetsov, said a few of his guys have screwed up a couple of her transports. Said they're all a bunch of violent thugs with no sense in their big dumb heads. And that's a direct quote."

"Does she know how dangerous he is?"

Skye nodded. "I've set up another meeting with her tonight just to reiterate things and to go over some details. She knows the deal. She's not doing anything that can get herself hurt or caught. She's just doing recon from afar and using some of her assets to keep tabs on some of his shipments. If that extra intel Hazel gave you is right, then Kuznetsov is bringing over a bunch of people and weapons in the next nine days, and he's using one of the ports in New Orleans—so he'll be in town."

Leighton had no reason to doubt the information. He was surprised Hazel had given it to him, but he'd learned that she wasn't the straightest arrow. Which, in a world full of gray, wasn't necessarily a bad thing. They weren't planning on doing anything about the incoming shipments—that was the Feds' job to handle. But if for some reason the FBI dropped the ball, they'd make sure this information fell into the right hands. There was always the DEA or even the CIA.

"Make sure she keeps her head down." He didn't like the thought of anything happening to the smart-ass smuggler. And it seemed that most people who tangled with Kuznetsov got dead fast.

"I've got a few places in New Orleans we can use," Brooks said, speaking for the first time as he typed something into his phone. "A couple homes in the Garden District that aren't listed under my name. They're owned by one of my dad's corporations. And unless Kuznetsov has a really deep file on me, he won't know about these homes."

"We?" Leighton asked, frowning.

Brooks lifted his head, pinning him with his dark eyes. "Yeah, we. Even if you're the one going to be on the ground at the casino, we're all going on this job. No one is working anything else right now and we need to help bring Kuznetsov down any way we can. If we can save one girl, we can save all of them. The Feds can do whatever the hell they want, but I'm not sitting by now that we have this information."

"I guess I could use the backup," he said, half-smiling. The truth was, this was the kind of job they all needed to be there for. There could be no room for error.

"Please. You need all the backup you can get, old man."

He snorted. He was less than six months older than Brooks. Instead of responding, Leighton looked at the screen again and frowned at the image of Luciana Carreras, the beautiful woman smiling at something just off camera. Her smile was wide and inviting. And her eyes...the bright blue was startling against her bronze skin.

If she was involved in her uncle's organization, it seemed even worse somehow because she was a woman. Sure, Gage said she might not be entrenched in Kuznetsov's bullshit, but Leighton couldn't believe it. There was no way she wasn't involved. She'd basically been raised by him, was college educated, worked at one of his hotels, and if women were being moved through there, she would have to know. She was the executive hotel manager.

And she was going down just like her uncle was.

CHAPTER TWO

—Intuition doesn't lie.—

Lucy stepped onto the main floor of The Sapphire where she managed. It was only ten in the morning but things were already hopping. That was just the nature of this job. Actually, that was the nature of the city in general. She'd moved to New Orleans when she'd taken over management here, and she'd discovered that the time of day basically didn't matter. There was always something going on.

Some days she contemplated looking for another management position, someplace where she didn't work for family. She'd been offered multiple different jobs after she'd graduated at the top of her class with a degree in business and hotel management—and landed a coveted intern position—but family was family, and her uncle had offered her this job. The pay and benefits were good, and a very small part of her, the little girl who'd been taken in by her uncle after her parents had died, felt a loyalty to him.

He was certainly an enigma though. She'd seen him viciously angry with some of the people who worked for him, to the point where he'd shoved a guy against a wall, but he'd never shown her that side. With her, he was always kind and gentle. But now she'd seen the other side of him and it was difficult to reconcile the two. Almost like Jekyll and Hyde.

Mentally, she shook herself. She wasn't sure what was wrong with her this morning. Okay, that was a big fat lie. The anniversary of her parents' deaths was coming up this week and she was feeling morose. But there was no time for that in the hospitality business. So she hid her private pain and pasted on a bright smile as she strode across the shiny floor, her Louboutins clicking away as she made her way to the concierge area.

Before she'd reached it, Anna Williams approached her, appearing as if out of nowhere. In reality, she'd come from one of the nearby doors that blended in with the wall. This hotel was like that, with paneled doors everywhere. She'd been in other casinos with the same setup and liked it. Made it easy to move around the hotel using back hallways.

Wearing the standard white pants and matching top that looked similar to hospital scrubs, Anna smiled as she reached Lucy. Even in heels, Lucy was the same height as her. Because her four-inch heels brought her up to a whopping five feet four inches. The increase in height seemed to help because some of the men she worked with liked to treat her like some fragile doll. It was annoying as hell—but not unexpected. She'd been dealing with it her entire life.

"I received the gift card and champagne," Anna said, her grin widening. "It was unnecessary but appreciated. So appreciated!" Her grin grew even wider. "My husband and I already drank it. It was like liquid gold."

"You deserved it after last week," she said. "And we appreciate all the hard work you do here."

Anna ran their exclusive spa efficiently, making sure every guest had a perfect experience. Last week, one of the high rollers' wives, who was known for being hard to deal with, had run the team ragged. Which was why Lucy had made sure Anna and all of her girls were taken care of. They were paid well—more than industry standard—but she still liked to do something extra when called for. Thankfully that particular high roller usually came to town solo. Lucy didn't understand treating anyone like garbage simply because you could. But that woman had no such issue.

So the small, really petty part of Lucy didn't feel bad that she'd heard through the grapevine that the woman's husband was leaving her.

"I know you're busy, I just wanted to thank you in person," Anna said.

"Any time. We've got a couple high rollers coming in next week. I'll get with you about some special services we're going to offer even to people who aren't staying here," Lucy said as she continued on toward the concierge desk. As she stepped up behind it, ready to check on one of their guests, out of the corner of her eye, she saw Marco emerge from one of the paneled doors into the lobby.

Instantly her back straightened even as she purposely didn't look in his direction. He didn't work at the hotel, but for her uncle instead. Her uncle wasn't in New Orleans most of the year, but Marco was, and he seemed to have full rein at the hotel, with a master keycard and everything.

When she'd questioned her uncle about what Marco's position was exactly, Uncle Alexei had been vague and said the man helped oversee some of his businesses. But Marco seemed to have a working relationship with some of the men on security here as well, which annoyed her. They were always having hushed conversations that ended when she came near. Sexist bullshit.

She was pretty sure it was because she was a woman and they all assumed she'd gotten her job because of nepotism. Which in a way she had, but she was more than qualified and could leave it anytime she wanted to pick up another job. When it came down to it, she'd known guys like this her entire life, who thought she should be home cooking for her man, barefoot and pregnant. She'd actually heard Marco say as much about her—that she shouldn't be working so hard, that she should be home making babies. *Gross.*

Her own mother had been a stay-at-home mom—and she respected any woman's right to do that—but her mother's relationship with her father had been special. Her mom had gotten to choose. She'd wanted to stay home, and things had been good between her parents.

Until they apparently hadn't.

Nope. Not going there right now. Her heart couldn't take it.

Out of the corner of her eye, she saw Marco making his way toward her, but tuned him out. The guy was such a Neanderthal, and when he looked at her, she

COVERT GAMES | 27

wanted to go take a shower. Or three. She'd never voiced her concerns to her uncle because she didn't like to make waves but seeing Marco put her on edge automatically. And she could never figure out what it was about him that bothered her. She'd seen him with women before. Truly stunning women. And they'd all looked miserable. Or maybe just hungry. She wasn't sure. Maybe that was what it was. Ugh, who cared. The guy was a douche, and she wasn't going to let him take up any more space in her brain.

She quickly logged into the concierge computer, nodding at Nathan, who was helping a guest, as she did. Mrs. Fisk hadn't checked out yet. Good. The older woman was one of their big spenders and one of Lucy's favorite guests. She always gave Lucy little candies and it reminded her of her mother. Lucy had a small gift she wanted to give the woman before she left.

"Lucy." The sound of Marco's voice grated against her senses. All around them, the ding-ding of machines going off in the casino, people chattering away in the lobby and beyond, and his voice, made her want to put earplugs in.

Looking up, she pasted on that fake smile she knew held a hint of frost. There was only so much faking a girl could do. "Hello."

"You look lovely this morning, princess."

Ugh. Gross. "Hmm," she murmured noncommittally as she glanced down at her phone, reading an incoming text from one of the concierges a few feet away. *Want me to save you with a fake emergency?* She stifled a giggle. Nathan knew how much she couldn't stand Marco.

"One of the security team told me you had an issue with a guest," Marco continued.

She frowned, tucking her phone back into her skirt pocket. "What?" And more importantly, who had told him? It certainly wasn't his business.

"Last night, one of the guests was harassing you."

She paused, trying to think of who he could be referring to. "Ah, one of the high rollers tried to get a little handsy. But I dealt with it." The guy had been slightly drunk—or more likely on some kind of prescription meds, because they'd stopped serving him—and he'd gotten a little fresh. If there was one thing her uncle had made sure she knew, it was self-defense. Not that she'd needed it to defend herself. Not with that drunk fool.

"You are Alexei's niece. If that happens again, you should—"

"I'll do what I did last night. Handle it. Your concern is noted but not necessary. I don't work for you. Now if you'll excuse me, I've got things to take care of." She turned away from him, ignoring his sound of protest. The casino had a ton of security and by the time two of the guys had stepped in, she'd already had the guy back in his seat and apologizing for his rude behavior.

"Lucy—"

Her phone started ringing, making her inwardly smile as she gave Marco a decidedly not apologetic look and held it to her ear. "You are a lifesaver," she murmured as she pulled open the nearest door that led to the maze of hallways in this place. Later, she'd have a talk with security about what they could and could not divulge to Marco about her, but for now she shelved all thoughts of the annoying man.

"So it's okay I'm calling this early?"

The sound of her young cousin's voice made her smile. Liliana was Uncle Alexei's daughter—and she was at the same English boarding school that Lucy had been shipped off to so many years ago. Liliana's half-brother had been allowed to go to school in the States. Something that had never sat well with Lucy. Not that she was close to her other cousin anyway. She hadn't spoken to him in years, though she did receive the obligatory Christmas card every year.

"It's not early. And you can call any time of day." Something the young girl already knew. "What's going on?"

"Nothing...just...I miss you. I want to come home."

Lucy rubbed her temple as she stepped around a maintenance worker. She continued east, needing to stop by one of the kitchens about a complaint she'd received. Then she was going to head up to the security floor. She could faintly hear the thump of music from one of the floors overhead, but these back hallways were insulated well. "I know. You're only there a few more years. And we'll see you for Christmas." After multiple kidnapping attempts on Liliana, Uncle Alexei didn't even let Liliana come home for holidays. They always went to her, usually meeting her in another location like Switzerland. He always said it was easier to keep her secure overseas. Liliana's half-brother never met with them. And Lucy knew he rarely called his sister either. He'd distanced himself completely and she wasn't sure why. Liliana snorted softly. "Last time I talked to Dad, he made it sound like I couldn't ever come home, like I should start university over here instead. I feel like he hates me some days."

"Oh, honey, that's not true. He just worries about your safety. Especially after what happened a few years ago." Lucy thought he was a bit overprotective, but Liliana had been targeted more than once because of his wealth. Assholes wanted to claim a ransom and hurt an innocent child in the process. Even though she could understand her uncle's protectiveness, deep down, she did judge him for how distant he kept Liliana. The girl had never known her mother at all. Lucy hadn't either. She just knew that the woman had abandoned Liliana.

"I guess. It's just…I'm the only kid who never goes home. Like, never. This doesn't feel normal to me. And it's not like I'm the only one here who's been the target of a kidnapping."

Since she was nearing the kitchen door, Lucy stopped and leaned against one of the walls. She could feel a headache coming on. She knew Liliana went to school with the daughters of other very wealthy people so the attempted kidnapping thing, while disturbing, wasn't exactly surprising. "I'm sorry. You want me to talk to him? Because you're right. You should be able to come home when you want. He'll be able to keep you safe. Heck, we can keep your trip a secret. And if he says no, you can come stay with me." Lucy knew exactly how that would go over. She'd always put up with her uncle's rules growing up because he'd taken her in and raised her. His son had already been out of the house by then. Not that it would have mattered; he'd sent Lucy off to school too. But when Liliana came along, Lucy had instantly bonded with her cousin. Unfortunately, most of their communication these days was phone calls, texting or video chats.

"You don't mind?"

"Of course not. We'll just have to use some of his security." Or more likely, a lot of it. Lucy didn't care though. It would be totally worth it.

"He'll be pissed if you tell him I can stay with you."

"So? He'll get over it."

"I don't know, Lucy..." Liliana sighed. "Do you ever think Dad..."

"Think what?"

There was a beat of silence. Then, "Nothing. I'm just mad at him right now. Don't worry about asking him. I don't want to put you in a weird position."

God, she sounded so grown-up for a fourteen-year-old. "I'm going to talk to him. But enough about that. How's school? And how was that concert?"

Liliana laughed lightly, the sound music to Lucy's ears. For the next few minutes, she shoved out all thoughts of this week being the anniversary of her parents' deaths, of Marco's creepiness, and her own growing loneliness.

Her cousin was a bright spot in her life, and she wasn't going to let her own crap drag anyone else down.

CHAPTER THREE

—Marriage to him is the greatest adventure of all.—

L eighton opened the door to the nondescript four-door sedan he and Savage were using this evening and slid into the front seat. The dome light didn't come on since Savage had already turned it off.

They'd all arrived in New Orleans a couple hours ago and had hit the ground running. That was the great thing about having a private jet at your disposal. Made travel a hell of a lot easier. They'd also procured various vehicles they'd be using while here.

"Her condo was a bust," Leighton said before Savage could ask him. He'd snuck into Luciana's condo. The security was more than decent, but not good enough to withstand Gage and Leighton's skills. She needed to replace her locks regardless. Gage had disabled the actual security system, but he'd picked her locks with surprising ease.

"Nothing?" Savage asked.

"No. No laptop, but I saw the cord for one on her desk. She likely takes it with her to work." There were a few other electronics, like an MP3 player and e-reader, but nothing he could use for their purposes. And he hadn't found any other weaknesses that might allow Gage to infiltrate the casino's security. There were other employees they thought about targeting, but she was potentially the best option since Kuznetsov was her uncle and she was an executive manager at The Sapphire. It stood to reason she'd have access to everything they would need.

"I'm surprised he doesn't have more security on her, considering most of the world doesn't even know about the existence of his daughter." Kuznetsov kept the daughter's existence vault-quiet but let Luciana work with him for all the world to see. Sure, they had different last names, but it didn't take much digging to find out they were related. And it wasn't as if Kuznetsov kept the fact of their familial tie a secret.

"She's his niece," Savage said absently as he steered out of the parking spot. They'd parked across the street from her condo complex. "That's different than a daughter."

"He should still increase her security. She could be a target." For some reason it bothered Leighton that her security wasn't as tight as it should be for someone related to a man like him. He shouldn't care at all but it annoyed him. Especially since Kuznetsov had raised her. The man should take better care of his family.

"It's good for us anyway," Savage said. "Does she have any safes or anything?"

"One in her closet. It was open." He nearly snorted at that. It was as if she'd opened it for something, then half-ass closed it. It hadn't quite clicked into place so he was able to peek inside. "Just personal papers and what looks like some heirloom-type jewelry. I took pictures of everything in case Gage can use it." They'd have been able to break in later and see what was inside but it had saved him time.

"Oh, he called while you were up there. He said she's leaving her volunteer position now and headed into work, according to her phone's location."

Gage had discovered that she volunteered at a suicide hotline. Her own father had killed her mother then killed himself. So that was likely the reason why. Her volunteer work made Leighton question whether she was as evil as her uncle, but sometimes there was no explaining why people did what they did. The psychology of why she was volunteering was pretty damn obvious. That didn't mean she couldn't have a darker side, couldn't be neck-deep in everything her uncle was.

"You ready for tonight?" Savage asked.

"Of course." He ignored the sideways glance his life-long friend shot him. He was getting tired of the way everyone looked at him. As if he was broken. Just because he didn't laugh or joke around like he used to didn't mean he was broken. He was just different. Life changed. People changed. Every single one of their group should know that. He wasn't some young kid anymore who thought he was invincible.

"Hey, thanks for Valencia's new backpack," Savage said as he took a left at the next stoplight.

Construction in this part of the city was ridiculous. Hell, most of the roads in and around the French Quarter were insane.

He lifted a shoulder. "No problem. I saw the unicorn on it and thought of her." He didn't know jack about kids but he knew that Savage's daughter loved unicorns, rainbows, and pretty much anything related to princesses or tiaras. Though lately she'd been very interested in pickpocketing, thanks to Skye's tutelage. "So how is everything, post marriage?"

"Kind of the same. Actually, it's better," Savage said. "There's something to be said for making everything official."

Leighton figured it mattered to Savage since he'd officially adopted Valencia. He could understand and respect that. He was pretty certain that marriage and kids and all that stuff wasn't in the cards for him but he was happy for his friend. All of his friends.

Sometimes it was hard not to feel like the outsider, however. They were all his family, but now that everyone was settling down, sometimes he could admit that he was more aware of his loneliness. But he shook that thought off. Right now he had a job to do, and that was to play the role of Spencer Johnson.

He could do pseudo-charming trust fund jackass, no problem.

* * *

"All right, let's go for ten in a row," Skye said, lifting the green grape in her hand.

Colt opened his mouth and waited as she aimed—and made it. Grinning, he chewed, then said, "What's the record?"

"I think, like, twenty, for that Idaho job. But I bet we can beat it today." She popped a grape in her own mouth before turning her attention to the vehicle across the street. Or more accurately, the man in the vehicle. "What kind of a name is Marco anyway? It seems too simple for this...monster." Or alleged monster, but please, the guy worked for Kuznetsov and had a fairly long criminal record. Mostly petty stuff when he was younger. Clearly he got smarter. Though he did have more than a handful of assault charges. Assault with a deadly weapon. Assault with intent to kill. And it just went on. But all of those charges were dropped. Because people "changed their minds." *Yeah, right.*

Colt simply made a noncommittal sound as he watched Marco Broussard, one of Kuznetsov's men, talk to a man they were pretty certain was a smuggler. Broussard's exact role in Kuznetsov's organization wasn't certain, but he appeared to look out for his New Orleans-based business interests.

"Open up," Skye said again, tossing another grape at her husband.

"That's eleven."

"So...Leighton seems like he's ready for this operation," Skye said into the quiet. Silences with Colt were never uncomfortable. Never had been. Not even from the beginning, when they'd still been getting to know each other.

"I think so too," her husband said.

Colt knew Leighton a lot better than Skye did. "I know you guys are worried about him but honestly, he just seems kind of lonely." Something most of the crew didn't seem to understand.

He shot her a surprised glance before looking back across the street, waiting for their mark to make a move. So far Marco had just been sitting talking to John Leroux, a man who'd been brought in by the New Orleans PD more than once on suspicion of transporting stolen goods. He'd never been charged, however.

"What?" Skye asked, snapping a picture of the two men together for their records. "Like that's so crazy? We've all basically paired off. And now Gage and Nova are engaged."

Colt made a sort of grunting sound. "Yeah. I never really thought about it. And I guess I kinda thought he'd end up with Hazel."

Skye snorted. "Those two? I know she's bisexual, but no way. They're way too much alike. Leighton needs someone different, maybe a little softer. In a way, he reminds me of Axel. I can totally see Leighton ending up with someone like Hadley." Once upon a time, Skye would have never imagined having a conversation like this. One that dissected their friends' relationships. It was all too...complicated and weird. But she'd finally accepted that she *had* friends. And these friends were more like her family now. That meant she cared and had opinions.

Colt just made that grunting sound. They'd been together long enough that she knew what his grunts meant. Right now, he disagreed with her.

"You'll see that I'm right. Because I'm always right," she added.

"Is that so?"

"Yep. At least you had the good sense to marry someone as smart as me."

Colt laughed aloud then and reached across the center console, taking one of her hands in his. They were rarely affectionate during operations, wanting to keep their heads solely focused on whatever job they were working on. Then they'd screw like maniacs once they had downtime. But she'd come to learn that her husband needed that extra affection sometimes. And she was learning to give it freely.

Because she would give Colt anything he wanted. The man had made her feel alive from the moment they'd met. He'd never made her doubt who she was, never made her feel different—even when she knew she didn't respond to many situations the way most people did. She also knew that most men wouldn't be secure enough to be with a woman like her. She understood that. But Colt...he was truly her North Star. And that was about as fucking poetic as she was ever going to get.

"Oh, he's moving," she said, even though he could see the same thing she could. Skye slid her earpiece in and turned it on. "Gage, you there?"

There was a short pause. "Yeah, what's up?"

"You find anything new on that Leroux guy?"

"How long have we worked together, Skye?"

"Years...give or take."

"And you still feel the need to ask me questions like that? You owe me a pizza."

"Fine. I'll make sure it has extra pineapple on it."

"You've got problems if you think fruit belongs on pizza... And yes, I've compiled a list of known associates that Leroux and Broussard have in common. Leroux doesn't work for Kuznetsov that I can tell, but he does do some smuggling for him. Basically contract work, but he's not loyal to the Russian. Just...I can't tell if he moves people or not." Frustration was clear in Gage's voice. "So far it just seems like he moves stolen stuff. For rich assholes."

So he might be useless for their purposes. They needed to figure out who Kuznetsov used for trafficking people in and around New Orleans. That person would lead them to the girl. Of course, that was if they couldn't find her at one of Kuznetsov's hotels. They were covering all their bases now, trying to find her—and any others they could. "Thanks, Gage."

He made a noncommittal sound, then, "You guys manage to tag his car?"

"No. We haven't been able to get close enough," Colt said. "Besides, from what I can tell, he's hired a driver. Maybe the guy works for Kuznetsov's organization or maybe it's really just a hired service. The company looks legit though." They'd already sent Gage all the details of the name of the company that'd picked up Broussard. Putting a tracker on the car would do nothing because the vehicle was going to end up back at the same place where it had started.

"All right. Let me know if you need anything else. I'm going to be monitoring Leighton for now."

"Thanks." Skye narrowed her gaze on Marco's vehicle as they followed after him, and imagined choking the shit out of him. It seemed too much that he would lead them directly to a bunch of trafficked women, but she could hope.

For now, they were going to follow their leads and do their best to find Hazel's family friend.

CHAPTER FOUR

—Remember, life is not a fairy tale.—

"Tell me what you've got," Lucy said quietly to Nathan. He was her extra set of eyes and ears, and he wasn't friendly with Marco, which was a big plus. She actually trusted Nathan.

"His name is Spencer Johnson. Comes from family money, but seems to have done well with his money on his own. Through investments and real estate. I can't know for sure but he might be in town on business. This is his first time here. Normally when he gambles, it's in Vegas or Atlantic City. But he has been to Biloxi at least on one occasion. Just never New Orleans. Or more accurately, he hasn't been at The Sapphire."

Lucy glanced around the floor, taking in the sights and sounds. Some people were dressed to the nines, as if they were going to the opera, while others wore velour track suits. Of course, there were at least two bachelorette parties enjoying themselves tonight. It was the weekend, so they usually had one—or half a dozen—bachelor or bachelorette parties coming through here. The casino had a dress code, but it was New Orleans, so occasionally they let some things slide.

"Sometimes it scares me how well you dig up stuff on people."

Nathan laughed once. "This was all just surface stuff. I barely dug anything up on this guy at all. Trust me, anyone here could've found this stuff out."

Nathan was self-deprecating but he actually sounded as if he was telling the truth this time. Still, she didn't go around digging up things on people, so it was all impressive to her. No, she didn't even have social media accounts. Naturally the casino did, and she checked in at least once a week to make sure it was being run properly because she understood how things that went viral could get out of hand quickly. But her uncle had been so adamant when she'd been younger that she not have *any* social media, and he was the same way with his daughter. His influence had just stuck with her. Anytime she thought about starting an Instagram account, she could hear his voice in her head telling her it was stupid and that her personal life was just that, personal. That the more she shared, the more it gave people ammunition to hurt her. Considering someone had tried to kidnap his daughter more than once, she could understand his concern.

"What kind of money is he spending?" she asked, shelving thoughts of her uncle's influence on her life.

"Midlevel now, but he's just getting started, I believe. He's losing and seriously doesn't seem to care. A quick scan of his financials—which, yes, did take more than a surface look—tells me he can afford to have a good time here."

"Any other vices I should know about?" There were only a few things that she wouldn't tolerate in the hotel. Something Nathan very well knew.

"Not that I could find," he said.

She nodded once. *Good.* "Why don't you get out of here? It's pretty late and you've put in more than a full day." She knew he should have left an hour ago, but he'd stuck around because she'd asked him to look into this new guy throwing a decent amount of money around. Nathan got paid overtime, but still, she wanted to respect his time. "You can come in late tomorrow too."

"You don't need to tell me twice. I've got a hot date lined up."

She snorted. When didn't he? "Kyle?"

He grinned. "Kyle and Marta."

She blinked once, but knew she shouldn't be surprised. Nathan was such a player that she never knew who he was coming and going with. "Have fun, then."

"Oh, I will," he said, heading out with a wave.

Lucy glanced down at her iPad and scanned more of the information Nathan had given her on this Spencer Johnson. She always paid attention to new people who appeared as if they'd be big spenders.

Lucy smiled at the blackjack dealer as she approached the table the dealer was currently shutting down.

"Mr. Johnson," she said, smiling at Spencer Johnson. "I believe this is your first time at The Sapphire. I'm Lucy Carreras, the executive manager here."

The man turned to look at her and she got the full effect of him. When Nathan had told her that he came from family money, she'd made the assumption that he was some trust fund kid—and she'd pictured him somehow younger. And softer. She'd only seen him from the back, and looking at him now he was definitely all man. With dark hair, a structured jawline and dark, haunted eyes, he pinned her in place for a solid moment before she managed to shake herself out of whatever was going on with her.

He left his chips on the table as the dealer said, "Would you like me to move your chips to table twenty?"

Mr. Johnson nodded and slid the guy a hundred dollar chip as a tip, but kept all his intense focus on Lucy. When he stood, she realized how tall he was. At least six feet. Give or take. It was difficult to tell since she was wearing her favorite five-inch, black-studded Valentino heels tonight.

"This is my first time in the casino, though not my first time in New Orleans. And I definitely would have remembered meeting you." He didn't speak in that charming, schmoozing way she was used to. He said it matter-of-factly as he held out a hand. And he had a buzz cut that reminded her of military guys. The cut definitely fit his strong face.

She shook his hand once, keeping her smile in place as she registered the calluses on his palms. Half the time she had to fake smiles at work for the customers. While she loved her job, dealing with some wealthy men and women was exhausting because of the way they treated people. But so far, no fake smiles for Mr. Johnson.

"Thank you for being so accommodating with us and moving to another table."

He lifted a shoulder. "I can lose or win at another table just as well as this one." He fell in step with her as they started walking across the casino floor.

Lucy noticed that he slowed, matching his stride with hers. "How long are you in town?"

"A week at least but my time is open-ended right now, so maybe longer."

"I see you're in one of our executive suites. Our Presidential Suite just opened up, and I'd like to offer it as a comp during your stay if you would like." Of course he wasn't going to say no.

He didn't look surprised at her offer, just nodded and smiled. "That sounds great, thank you. How long have you worked here?"

This question took her off guard. Patrons rarely asked her personal questions. Which was just fine with her. She was here to do a job. "Two years."

"Well, it's a great hotel. I've heard very positive things about management."

Despite herself, she found her cheeks flushing slightly. She had improved business since taking over. Her uncle had put a total moron in charge for the first year the casino had been open, but as soon as she'd taken over she'd made a lot of changes. It was a casino—it was easy enough to make money. But unless you had the right people running things, you could also lose a ton. Because hotels themselves were very expensive to run.

"Thank you," she said as they reached the new table. "If you need anything, just let me know." She handed him her business card, which included her cell phone number. Well, the cell phone number used for clients, not her normal cell phone. That was reserved for friends.

"Would it be totally inappropriate if I asked you out to dinner?" he asked, fairly abruptly.

Because there really wasn't a way to transition into that.

"I don't generally mix business and pleasure, so if you're asking me out on a date, then the answer is unfortunately no."

"Fair enough. What if I wanted to take you to lunch and to learn a bit more about the city from an insider? I'm thinking about buying some property here. It's the reason I'm in town. And while I trust my real estate agent, I'm curious what a local thinks."

Lucy was pretty certain he was still asking her on a date, but...he seemed sincere. Although the truth was, she found herself intrigued by those dark, haunted eyes. His outward appearance was strong, built, and so very muscular—there were some things a suit jacket couldn't hide. But his eyes were what drew her in. He appeared almost sad. "I think I can manage one lunch. As long as it's not at the casino and as long as you understand that this is just a professional meeting. I'll take you to a local place in the Quarter."

He nodded once, something a lot like interest sparking in those dark eyes. "How about tomorrow?"

Gah, what the heck was she doing? It wasn't as if it was against hotel policy to get involved with customers. Well, not technically. She nodded once. "Just call my cell phone. We'll set something up. And to be clear, this is definitely not a date." She didn't smile as she said it, keeping her voice firm.

He smiled at her, and she saw just a tiny hint of sensuality peeking through.

Only when she stepped away from him was she able to breathe again. She started across the casino floor and swore she could feel his eyes burning into her back.

To her left, she heard someone shouting as they won one of the slot machine payouts. She glanced in that direction and, against her better judgment, turned back around.

To her surprise, he was watching her walk away with a very heated stare.

She quickly glanced away, not wanting to get pulled in by those eyes again. Seriously, what the hell was going on with her? She got asked out all the time. Daily. Usually by jackasses either here or in her non-work life. She was able to brush off date requests, no problem, able to brush off men in general with no problem.

She knew why too. God, she'd thought her parents had the perfect marriage, that they were fairy-tale happy. But she'd just been a stupid kid who'd apparently not been able to see the darker side of their relationship. Some days, she wondered how she hadn't seen that something was wrong. Even when she racked her brain, trying to think of something she'd missed...there was nothing. Her father had completely worshipped her mother. And he'd been a doting father who had no problem spoiling both her and her mom.

Then he'd killed her mother and then himself.

Her entire childhood had been a lie. She must have just built their relationship up in her head, imagined how happy they'd all been.

She swore she'd never do that to herself. Never let a man lie to her, pull the wool over her eyes. Dating was fine, though she rarely did that with how busy she was. Marriage and relationships, however? No, thank you. Not that she had any reason to be thinking of that anyway.

Shaking off thoughts of the sexy, rich man with callused hands and sad eyes, she pulled out her work cell phone and checked in with security. She had a busy night of work and definitely did not need a distraction of the male variety.

* * *

"How you doing?" Leighton asked Gage through his earpiece, keeping his tone low. Not that it mattered. The casino was loud and seemed to be getting louder every minute that passed. He was fine being here for an op, but holy shit this would wear on him day in and day out.

Thankfully the place was smoke free, but the constant chatter, shouts of glee, groans of distress, and never-ending *ding, ding, ding* sound of the slot machines was maddening. Not to mention more than one woman had rubbed up on him as he'd played blackjack.

He liked his space and didn't appreciate people touching him without permission. But he brushed it off, acting as if he didn't care.

"More than good. Managed to clone the manager's phone. One of them anyway."

"One of?"

"Yeah. His niece has got two phones on her person. I cloned one because the security is shit. I've also been able to hack into a couple employees' phones and use them to my advantage. Managed to infiltrate part of their security system."

"Seen anything good?" Casually, he headed toward the cashiers' cage, ready to turn in his leftover chips. He'd lost a lot tonight, which was good for his cover.

"Maybe. I don't have access to all the cameras. Just a few of the exterior of the hotel and none on the actual casino floor. They've got the hotel and casino set up on different systems. It's interesting."

Interesting could be good or bad.

"I'm pretty sure this is a security oversight someone missed during an update and I'm taking full advantage." Gage started muttering to himself then, and Leighton figured he'd lost his friend for a while at least as he worked.

After turning in the chips and getting cash back, he headed to one of the cocktail bars. There were a few empty seats, but he didn't want to have to deal with bull-shit small talk with anyone, so he chose a single seat in between two separate couples. No one would bother him this way.

"What's Nova up to?" he murmured even as he motioned to the bartender. The place was so loud that no one would be able to overhear him talking to Gage. If anything, they would assume he was talking into a Bluetooth. And in his experience, people were so self-involved they wouldn't be paying attention anyway.

"What... Oh, she's sleeping. She's insisting on helping with one of the recon missions tomorrow." There was frustration in Gage's voice.

Leighton understood, because he wasn't sure how he would deal with having a significant other who was part of their world. He'd probably worry all the time. Unless of course his significant other was someone like Skye. Then he'd just worry for the rest of the world. But...she wasn't remotely his type. Hell, he didn't know what his type was.

And he was annoyed as fuck that he found himself seriously attracted to Luciana Carreras. She had curves in all the right places, full breasts that should be too big for her petite frame, but simply looked perfect under that sexy black and white dress she'd been wearing earlier. Damn, and he'd only seen her with clothes on. Imagining what she'd look like naked was... Damn it. *Not* something he needed to be doing. He'd just asked her out as part of their failsafe plan to get close to her if necessary. If Gage couldn't work his magic.

For some reason, he couldn't stop thinking about how soft her hand had been in his when he'd taken it in his much bigger one. Or how her bottom lip was bigger than her top, giving her a perpetually pouty look—or how her bright blue eyes had seemed to see straight through to his soul.

Fuck him. He lifted up the bar menu and pointed to the beer he wanted as the bartender headed over. The guy simply nodded and grabbed one for him.

Leighton cleared his throat, taking the beer the bartender set in front of him as he said, "She's more than capable."

"Yeah, I know. Still don't have to like her being on this op."

"You'd prefer her to be at home, hundreds of miles away?"

There was a pause, then, "No."

"All right, then," he said, taking a swig of his beer. "Be glad your girl is here with you."

Gage just made an annoyed mutter, the sound of the keyboard clacking away in the background. "Hey, I think I might have something. I ran a facial recognition... You know what, never mind. But one of Kuznetsov's men is definitely at the casino now. And I'm talking one of his actual guys, not the random people he has working for him in various cities."

"Where is he?" Leighton tossed a bill onto the bar and stood, his body practically vibrating with the thump of the music over the speakers.

"Second floor, entering a stairwell. Ah...west side of the hotel."

So, opposite of where Leighton was. He wasn't going to race over there for no reason. "What's he doing?" he asked, heading toward the elevators. He'd have to stop talking once he got in the elevator on the chance it was being monitored. It definitely *was* being monitored in the general sense, but there was also a chance security wouldn't be listening in unless they had a good reason. Their main concern was making sure people weren't stealing or doing other illegal stuff. But mainly, they were concerned with the security aspect of the casino.

"Give me a sec," Gage murmured.

"All right. Getting in the elevator."

"Okay...guy's name is Misha Popov. He's in the top tier of Kuznetsov's organization. Whatever the reason he's here, it can't be good. Probably why the Feds are in town. He's leaving out a side exit. I'll tail him using CCTVs if possible. Gonna check in with Skye and Colt. Hang tight."

As he rode up to his room, Leighton waited as Gage added them onto the comm line. He wanted to leave and join the others, but on the off chance he was being watched, he didn't want to do anything suspicious.

Sometimes that was the hard part about these operations, having to stick to one part of the op when he wanted to get involved with everything.

CHAPTER FIVE

—You know the truth by the way it feels.—

L ucy rubbed her temple as she strode across the casino floor. It was two in the morning and time for
her to get out of here. It was no wonder she had no social
life, given her crazy hours. As she headed for the west set
of elevators, she frowned when she saw a local man she
recognized well enough leaving the floor, his arm linked
with a tall, beautiful woman with brown skin and
model-long legs. She'd never seen the woman before but
she knew the man, Darius something. He lived in New
Orleans and normally came to the casino on Friday or
Saturday nights to play the craps tables. He'd never
stayed at this hotel. Would have no need to.

Frowning, she watched as the couple walked off together, clearly very enamored with each other. Or at
least he was enamored with her. Lucy didn't like to judge
based on appearances, but the woman was light years out
of Darius's league, and this was the third time she'd seen
him hooking up with a woman who looked like the
woman on his arm. Not physically exactly, but the same
type of woman—tall and beautiful.

Yes, there was definitely a chance he was simply getting lucky with out-of-town visitors, but she'd taken

courses on what to look for when it came to trafficking...and something did not sit right with her.

Instead of tagging security on her phone, she headed to the other set of elevators and went straight to the security floor, using her keycard to allow for full access. She should've looked into this earlier, but now that she was off work, she had all the time she needed.

On the security floor, she swiped her keycard against the glass doors and nodded once at Nick, the security manager on duty this weekend. She liked the older man well enough. He had a lot of experience and did his job well. He'd been with a casino in Vegas for a decade and had come highly recommended.

"Lucy, I'm surprised to see you here. Everything okay?"

"Yes. I'm just checking up on something. Do you have a free computer?"

He paused and then nodded. She wasn't his boss in the technical sense, but as far as the hierarchy went she was definitely ranked above him. Not that he had any reason to question her presence on this floor. It was slightly out of the ordinary but she had every right to be here.

"Come on, Jorge's office is empty right now. You can use his computer if you need. Is there anything I can help you with? I can probably find it a lot faster."

She half-smiled because it was true. But she understood how to do facial recognition searches using the parameters on their security system, and was comfortable doing the search herself. And she wasn't sure what to tell him just yet so she simply shook her head. "Thank you for the offer. I'm sure you have your hands full and this is definitely not a priority. I was just getting off work and thought I'd do something before heading home."

He nodded once. "Sure thing. Let me know if you change your mind. And if you're hungry, they just stocked our kitchen so there's plenty of food or whatever."

"Thanks," she said, sinking into Jorge's chair. She quickly typed in her own credentials then pulled up one of the programs she knew she would need.

Doing a search for the timeframe she'd seen Darius was easy, since he'd just left the main floor. She pulled up an image of his face, then did another search covering the last three weeks, wanting to be thorough. While the computer ran the program, she captured the face of the woman he'd been with and did a search on her as well.

Ping. Ping. The computer quickly fed her the information she'd requested on Darius. She pulled up the various video clips from different dates—and saw that on various evenings from the last few weeks, he'd been seen leaving with different women, heading up to their hotel rooms. Or she assumed so. She was going to check who'd rented the rooms as well.

From there, she captured images of each woman she'd seen him leaving with and did searches on them too. The biometric technology was fairly new and definitely wouldn't catch everything she wanted—it was better at working with neutral expressions and full faces, but she was going to see what she could find. Since she could see what floor they got off on—always the same one—it made her searches a bit easier.

It took time to gather the information, but she wasn't going anywhere until she got what she needed.

Once she'd gotten room numbers, she did more searches and found out that...the rooms they'd been using hadn't been occupied at the time of use. Well, technically they had been, but they were listed as free rooms.

Her stomach twisted at the knowledge. If Darius and these women were using rooms that were free, it meant someone who worked here had told them. Oh, this was not looking good.

When she didn't see any of the women in her searches other than the one time, she expanded the parameter and went back six months.

More waiting.

A few minutes later, she got another ping: this time three of the women showed up in different rotations, leaving with different men right around the two a.m. mark on different days. After a double-check of the rooms they'd used, she found that they'd all been listed as free.

She tapped her finger against the desk, frowning about what she was going to do with the information. As she thought about the ramifications of all this, she frowned slightly as she spotted a familiar face on one of the screens. Michael Atkins.

He often worked security.

He was on the floor, watching one of the women leave with a casino patron. She scrolled back to the different feeds with Darius and the different women. And Michael was in each one of them, watching, hanging out subtly in the background.

What was he, like a pimp or something? She didn't want to jump to conclusions but this was all too fishy. And she wasn't going to ignore it.

Now she was really glad she hadn't asked for help, because Michael was part of the security team. Though she hadn't hired him. He'd been here when she'd come on board. She had no particular feelings about him whatsoever. He did his job, but they often worked different shifts and she didn't interact with him more than necessary. But she was pretty certain her uncle knew him. And if her uncle found out what Lucy suspected Michael was up to, he would not like this.

Okay, forget being cautious, she was going to call her uncle and tell him what was going on. There was no way she was going to put up with this bullshit in the casino. This was the kind of thing that could get them raided or shut down. Not to mention if these women weren't engaged in their profession consensually, that was a whole other can of worms. If grown-ups wanted to trade sex for money, that was their business. As long as it was consensual and didn't interfere with *her* business. But she also knew that vulnerable women could be exploited, so she sure as hell wasn't going to let this go on any longer.

Running on fumes at this point, she saved all of the information to a flash drive and tucked it into her skirt pocket. As soon as she got home, she was going to chug some coffee and review the information again just to be sure before she called her uncle. She wouldn't be able to sleep until she talked to him.

* * *

Lucy tapped her finger against her kitchen countertop as her call went through. When she realized the time, she winced. It was close to four in the morning. *Damn it.* She should just hang up.

But then another surge of adrenaline punched through her as she thought about everything she'd discovered. She had no doubt that Mike was somehow involved with something—maybe not trafficking women, but he was at least involved in prostitution. And he was putting all of the casino at risk. Not to mention if she found out—

"Lucy." Her uncle's voice was intense. "Are you okay?"

"Yes. I'm sorry. I realized the time after I pressed call and—"

"It's not a problem. I've been awake for half an hour. You know me. The early bird catches the worm and all that."

She laughed lightly despite her dark mood. Her uncle often got idioms wrong so it made her smile that he got this one right. "I have something to tell you, and I know what I'm going to do. But...I'm not sure the extent of how involved I should get with this and what steps I should take to correct it. I'm certain that one of our employees is involved in running prostitution through The Sapphire."

Talking quickly, she laid out what she'd found out about Mike, the little details with the rooms being unused, and her suspicions overall.

"It's more than a suspicion though. I'm going with my instinct on this. Do I have one hundred percent proof? No. But I don't need that much proof. I've already sent an email to his supervisor letting her know to cancel all Mike's shifts. And I'm going to fire him." Since this was an at-will state she didn't need to worry about giving a reason. "And I know that we need to do an internal investigation because clearly someone else is involved. Or I assume someone is, because they have access to our rooms' vacancies and whatnot. Do we involve the police or what?"

Her uncle was silent for a long moment. Then he said, "It's good you came to me. I don't think we should involve the police. Because while I don't like prostitution in one of our casinos, I also don't want those women to be inadvertently arrested or involved."

That had been Lucy's thought process as well. She wasn't quite sure of the legalities of it but she knew that the women could be arrested, and her opinion of that was bullshit. If someone was exploiting or forcing the women, they were the ones who should be arrested. "Okay."

"Don't worry about firing him. I'll take care of it personally."

"You don't have to do that!" Lucy knew how busy he was. Even if he hadn't been her uncle, she still would've called him because he was the owner of the casino. "This is something I can handle on my own."

"I have no doubt that you can, but if Atkins is doing this at one of my casinos, there's no telling what else he's been involved in. I'm going to handle this, and I'll set up the investigation myself. It's not up for discussion."

She knew better than to argue when her uncle used that tone. And the truth was, she was glad she didn't have to deal with Mike. "Thank you. What about the women though? I want to help them if they need it." If they were in their profession voluntarily, Lucy would leave it alone, but they might need help, and she wouldn't be able to sleep if she didn't try to help.

Her uncle was silent again for a long moment. Finally he said, "I know a private investigator in the city. I'll bring him into our internal investigation and see if he can find out who the women are and any other details involving them. This is something I don't want you getting involved in, however. You were smart to come to me, but I don't want to hear that you're doing investigative work on your own."

"Okay, I won't." *Well, maybe.* But she didn't tell him that. She'd wait and see what happened with the investigation.

"Have you gotten any sleep?"

She let out a short laugh. "No. I came straight home and reviewed everything again then called you."

"You're doing a good job at the casino. I'm proud of you."

"Ah, thank you." Despite herself, she slightly preened under his praise, even though she knew it was ridiculous. But he'd been a father figure to her, replacing her own father. He might not have been overly warm or affectionate, but he'd given her every opportunity she could need in life to be successful. He'd taken care of her trust and looked out for her. Sure, he wasn't very complimentary and sometimes it was as if he was tossing her morsels of praise to appease her. And she was ashamed to admit she ate them up. Maybe she had issues. Clearing her throat, she said, "Listen, I talked to Liliana yesterday."

"Ah, my wonderful girl. How is she doing?"

It bothered Lucy that he even had to ask. He should *know*. He should talk to his daughter every week. More than once. "Good enough. School is going well. And she has good friends. She's staying out of trouble, which I'm sure you know." Because there was no doubt that her uncle had guards on his daughter. The school was secure but she knew her uncle well enough that he'd give Liliana extra security. The kidnapping attempts on her had really rattled him. "She wants to come home for the holidays."

He made a tsking sound. "I've already planned a vacation for all of us. We will go skiing in Switzerland."

"She doesn't want to go to Switzerland."

"Fine. We'll do something new this year. Maybe we'll go somewhere warm, to Australia. Wherever she wants."

Lucy sighed, even as she rubbed her temple. She was exhausted and knew this wasn't the time to have this particular conversation with her uncle. Maybe it was the exhaustion pushing her to run her mouth, however. "She wants to come home," Lucy said despite herself. "She needs to know she has an actual place to come home to. She hasn't been to the States in years. It's not good. It's not good for anyone to feel like they don't have roots." Jesus, Lucy should know. Some days—most days—she felt completely untethered to everything around her.

Her uncle sighed, the sound long and heavy. "You know how much I need to protect her."

"I do know. But the last attempt on her was five years ago. She's more aware of the danger now, of her surroundings. She's a smart girl. If anything, she can come here, stay with me for the holiday break. There's so much to do here that she would love. We can catch a play, see a couple concerts, the Christmas Eve bonfires… Liliana would love it." She bit her bottom lip as she waited for him to respond. He'd never been truly angry at her but she'd also never pushed back about much.

He sighed again. "Let's discuss this later. I have much work to do today. I'll call Liliana later and we'll figure something out. Thank you again for bringing this issue to my attention though. I promise to deal with it immediately. In fact, I'll be in town in a couple days so I'll update you then."

"That's great. I assume this is for business?" Because he wouldn't be coming just to see her.

"Yes. I've always got something to do." He laughed, though it sounded almost strained.

Or maybe she was just out of fumes at this point and ready to fall asleep on her feet. And she knew he would not be discussing anything with her later regarding Liliana. If she had to guess, he would call his daughter and convince her that she did not want to come home for the holidays.

Even if Lucy wanted to push the subject, now definitely wasn't the time. She needed to talk to him again when she was levelheaded and not dealing with a work crisis.

"I'll see you in a couple days, then. Thank you for handling this." She knew he was going to start an investigation but she was going to look through the rest of the security feeds and see if she could find anything else. Particularly if Mike had been working with anyone. She was going to make sure that if anyone else was involved, they'd be fired as well.

"Good." Then he disconnected without another word, which was definitely his way.

Sighing, she set her phone down and stood. She needed a shower and sleep.

CHAPTER SIX

—I never expected her.—

"You're clear," Gage said into Leighton's earpiece. Leighton didn't break pace as he strolled down the quiet street in the Garden District. He'd left the hotel an hour ago and gone on a faux tour of the city by himself, only coming to their safe house—one of them—once he knew he wasn't being tailed.

Gage had set up a security perimeter around the entire street. It was subtle and no one else would notice it, and they would remove most of the cameras when they left town, but it added an extra layer of security for all of them.

He opened up the wrought iron gate and instead of heading up to the front door of the three-story Victorian house, he walked along the side of it and headed around the back as he'd been instructed. Then he jumped up onto the raised back porch and opened the back door into the huge kitchen to find everybody eating and talking.

Gage had called a meeting and, since Lucy had texted him to move their lunch a little later, he'd jumped at the chance to see everybody in person and find out what the next plan of action was. Other than him hoping to find Hazel's family friend. He knew that Gage had cloned

Lucy's phone, so he had his fingers crossed that the hacker had found something interesting because he'd sounded excited when he'd called Leighton.

"You're acting like a child," Skye said even as she tossed a blueberry at Axel's head.

"It's not childish to miss your wife." The former hit man did look close to sulking, however, as he took the blueberry and popped it in his mouth.

Colt frowned at Skye. "Wait a minute, I thought you said Hadley—" Colt was cut off as Skye quickly kissed him.

"What did you say about Hadley?" Axel asked.

"None of your business," Skye said, returning to her plate. "Besides, you know she's safe and having a good time. She and Darcy are having sleepovers every night. They're probably doing each other's hair and having pillow fights. That should give you spank-bank material for, like, ever."

Axel snorted. "Women don't actually have pillow fights."

Skye lifted an eyebrow and took a handful of raspberries and dumped them on her plate. "Just shows how much you know about women."

Axel stilled for a long moment then said, "Wait a minute, are you serious about that? Do women really do that?"

Skye howled in laughter. "Oh my God. I think *you* get the name of 'dumbass' now instead of Gage."

"Hey!" Nova said from across the table, frowning over her glass of orange juice. "Only I get to call him that."

Gage shot a look at Leighton as he stepped farther into the room and simply shook his head as if exasperated with *all* of them. "Now that Leighton is here, we can finally get down to business. Have you eaten?" Gage asked.

He nodded, since he'd gotten breakfast at the hotel, but he headed for the coffee maker anyway. He clapped Savage on the shoulder once and murmured a greeting to the other man, who was being fairly quiet. Olivia had opted not to come on this mission because she hadn't wanted to be away from their daughter.

"As you guys know, I cloned Lucy's phone. And what we thought about her is definitely wrong. She's not involved in her uncle's operations. Or it would appear not, according to this."

He pressed a couple buttons on his laptop and then an audio feed streamed over the computer speaker. They were all quiet as they listened to the conversation she'd had with her uncle. According to Gage, she'd called her uncle around four in the morning. No wonder she'd moved their lunch back.

"Damn," Skye said as the conversation ended. "She doesn't seem to have any idea what a monster her uncle is. It's not like he's going to do an actual investigation. If anything, that Atkins guy was likely working for him. Or for Broussard."

"Yeah, no kidding," Leighton muttered. "Do you know who this guy is?" he asked, looking at Gage.

"Yeah. I ran a search on his name and started a file on him. Kuznetsov might just move him to another hotel or city. From what I can tell, the guy's lifestyle is slightly more lavish than it should be with what he makes doing security. But it's not obscene. He's not one of Kuznetsov's inner circle. Not even close. And he doesn't have a direct link to Kuznetsov. He appears to just be a local, lived here his whole life, so again, only guessing here, he was likely recruited to do some extra work and look the other way where these women are concerned. Probably not even recruited by Kuznetsov. I can't imagine him pulling in someone so small-time."

"We should still get eyes and ears on him," Colt said, pushing his plate away.

"Agreed," Savage said. "It sounds like he's being fired so I can tail him today, maybe plant a bug in his place or on his phone."

Colt nodded and the others started working out logistics of the day, while Leighton tried to get his head on straight.

Lucy wasn't at all who he'd assumed she was. And if she knew nothing about who her uncle was, if she found out, it was going to shock and upset her. But…he wondered if they could use that to their advantage.

Even as he had the thought, he felt sick. He didn't like using innocent people.

But in the end, they had to save Maria, had to save as many women as they could. Because despite what Lucy had seemed to think during the phone conversation with Kuznetsov, the women definitely weren't volunteering for anything.

* * *

The November weather was perfect as Lucy strolled down the sidewalk with Spencer Johnson. Thankfully he hadn't minded when she'd pushed their lunch back.

She'd taken him to one of her favorite local places and was pleased that he'd enjoyed it, and he'd been incredibly polite to the staff. It wasn't that she'd expected otherwise, but sometimes you never knew with people. And they usually showed their true selves when interacting with waitstaff. She'd cut more than one date short because a man had been rude to their waiter or waitress.

"I've never had chicken and waffles before. I never would have thought to put them together," Spencer said.

"It's one of my favorites," she murmured, looking over at a two-story revival-style home in the Garden District. He'd wanted to walk around here and she could admit she was enjoying the downtime. Not to mention her company was sexy and smart. And had sad eyes. God, his dark eyes were like this beacon, calling to her. "So is this real estate purchase for business or just for you?"

He lifted a shoulder, his very sexy mouth curving up just the slightest bit. "I'm undecided. Originally it was just supposed to be a business purchase. But it would be nice to own a home here."

She nearly snorted because, yeah, it would be incredible to own a home here, especially in the Quarter or Garden District. "I love it here." But the homes were so expensive. The truth was, if she asked her uncle, he would likely buy her a home in the Garden District. Or if she wanted to, she could actually purchase one with money from her trust, but she'd barely touched it since she'd come of age.

There were far too many reasons she hadn't touched it, none of which would make sense to anyone else but herself. But she liked paying for things with her own money. Well, money that she earned, because that money in the trust was hers as well. She shook those thoughts off because they had the ability to take her down a dark path. And that was the last place she wanted to be mentally right now.

"Where do you live?" he asked. "I mean, not your address obviously, but what part of town?"

"I'm in the business district. I would love to have a place here though. Or maybe even in the heart of the Quarter. But I fear I would literally never sleep if I lived there."

He chuckled softly and took her elbow gently as they stepped over an uneven section of sidewalk. An oak tree had grown up under it and was pushing the concrete pieces upward, little cracks spidering out in all directions.

Once they stepped over it, he didn't let go, and she found that she liked it. His hand was warm, strong, and gentle at the same time.

"It's certainly a party down here, isn't it?"

"It is during certain times of the year. And most of the Quarter is always busy and lively. But it's not like that everywhere. It's honestly just like anywhere else. People have their lives, take their kids to school, go to work…you know, just like everywhere."

"Maybe, but there's certainly a lot of history here."

"That's very true. It's one of the reasons I didn't mind moving here for my job."

"How did you end up with a job here, if you don't mind me asking? I know the hotel is pretty new."

She didn't like to tell people that her uncle was the owner, mainly because they made assumptions about how she got her job. "After college, I had a few offers and I ended up picking this one. There were a lot of reasons. The city is definitely one of them. I like the area and I like that there aren't really harsh winters here." Maybe if they got to know each other she would tell him about her familial relationship with the owner, but very likely this was just a casual lunch. For some reason, the thought of that made her a bit sad. And she wasn't sure why. She barely knew Spencer.

"Well, it's clear you're doing something right. At least that's what I've heard." His voice was butter smooth, all deep and sexy and doing strange things to her insides.

She could listen to him talk all afternoon. She was having a hard time remembering why she'd decided that this shouldn't be a real date. "Really?"

He nodded once. "I don't stay at a hotel unless I know about the management style."

That was a little surprising, but it also told her a lot about his own business style. It was smart, especially for a man who appeared to be quite wealthy.

"I probably should've asked this earlier," he continued. "And I know you said this is absolutely not a date. But I did want to ask if you're dating anyone?"

The question took her off guard as they reached the end of the street. "You're right, this isn't a date."

He grinned ever so slightly. "Well, for the record, I'm single. And I'm definitely not dating anyone." His words were matter-of-fact.

She shouldn't respond. Nope, she should just change the subject because this was definitely wading into personal territory.

"I'm not dating anyone either. Not that it matters," she tacked on. Part of her liked that he actually asked. And whether or not he was telling the truth about being single, she couldn't know for sure. But the file that Nathan had given her on Spencer Johnson indicated that he was very much single. And he was so straightforward about everything, she found she liked his demeanor. "I might change my mind about going on a date with you," she said, surprising herself.

It was clear she'd surprised him as well but he covered it quickly with a grin. Not a smug, obnoxious one but a very subtle, very sexy smile. He nodded once to the left and asked if that was the right direction.

Nodding, she fell into step with him and was pleased when he took her arm again. The sidewalk was uneven on this street as well. Mardi Gras beads still hung from trees even though Mardi Gras was in the beginning of the year. It didn't seem to matter. They were tossed about everywhere, year-round. She found she loved the sight of the bright beads glinting in the sunlight.

"So what changed your mind?" he asked, his voice dropping just an octave.

She shrugged, smiling. "You did."

"All right, then. I'll take it. How about I take you out tomorrow night?"

She wondered why he didn't ask about tonight, but then she remembered that she'd told him she was working. Clearly he listened when she spoke. "Perfect. I can meet you out somewhere. And since it's a date, you can pick the place. Unless you want me to?"

"I know you're the local, but I have a couple ideas."

"Sounds good." God, the man was sexy, and she liked that he was taking charge.

They stopped in front of one of the houses he'd wanted to see. He'd told her that later in the week, he had a day planned with his real estate agent to see places, but there was an open house on a place he wanted to visit today.

The four-foot-high gate was open and as they stepped through together, she tripped in her heels. That was what she got for going for the sexy footwear.

Spencer steadied her, his big hands moving to her waist as he pulled her close. She inhaled, noticing for the tenth time how good he smelled. And as she looked up into his dark, haunted eyes, she had the strongest urge to kiss him. Just lean up and press her lips to his and wipe away that sadness that seemed to linger.

"I really want to kiss you now," he murmured as if he'd read her mind.

"Yeah, well, the feeling is mutual," she whispered, instantly wincing. Normally she kept things locked down, but it was impossible to do so now. Or to care that this wasn't supposed to be a date as her fingers pressed lightly against his rock-hard chest. He was gripping her hips far too possessively, and she found she liked it just a little too much.

Taking her by surprise, he leaned down and gently brushed his lips over hers, his lips soft and perfect. He tasted like the after-lunch coffee they'd had, with just a hint of chocolate.

Before she could truly enjoy him, lean into him, he pulled his head back and let out a muted groan. "I should've waited until our date, but now I won't be obsessing over what you taste like."

There was something about the way he said taste that sent a surge of heat straight to her core. She wasn't some virgin but she felt her cheeks flush and her nipples tightening against her bra cups as they stood there staring at each other. What was this man doing to her?

She slid her hands up his chest, wanting another taste of him. A real one.

"Are you two here for the open house?" A female voice brought her back to reality, and she quickly stepped back from Spencer.

She wasn't some teenager making out in public with some guy she barely knew. Not that she'd ever done that anyway.

There are consequences to your actions. She could practically hear her uncle's words from her teenage years ringing in her head as he lectured her about staying away from boys.

Putting on a smile for the real estate agent who'd interrupted them, she let Spencer take the lead, since he was the one looking at the place. As he spoke to the woman, it gave her a moment to compose herself and get her head on straight.

Maybe...she could indulge in something with him. He didn't live here, so it would just be a fling. Which would be better for her in the end. She knew better than to have stupid emotional attachments.

Because people always disappointed you.

CHAPTER SEVEN

—Damn it.—

"I'm pretty sure I picked up a tail on the way back," Leighton said quietly into his phone. He was in the bathroom of the Presidential Suite with the shower running. He'd done a scan for bugs and other electronics and was certain he wasn't being listened to, but he was still taking extra precautions. Right now more than ever they had to be careful.

"Did you get a good look?" Colt asked.

"No. Just a feeling I've had before. Could be nothing but my instinct tells me otherwise. And I didn't get that feeling until I got close to the actual casino."

"Well, you did go out with Kuznetsov's niece. He or someone who works for him could be keeping an eye on you. But…do you need to pull out?" Colt asked, his tone deadly serious.

"I think if my cover was blown, I'd know." He'd already thought about it and he wanted to stay put. "I don't want to pull out yet. I want to scout the casino floor again at least one more night, see what we can pick up on cameras. Gage still hasn't completely infiltrated their system." And Leighton didn't think Kuznetsov would stop running women simply because his niece had stumbled onto a small portion of his operation. No, the asshole would just get smarter about it. Kuznetsov liked money too much.

"All right. We've all got your back regardless. And if something happens, I have no doubt you'll be able to fight your way out."

Leighton half laughed. "Glad you've got so much faith in me."

"So how was lunch with her? Did you get a better feel for her?"

Leighton wasn't certain how to answer that. He decided to go with the truth, however. "I really like her."

Colt was silent for a long moment. "Like her, like her? Or…"

"Like her, like her."

"You're serious." Colt's tone was neutral.

"Yeah. I kissed her. And I can tell myself that it was all part of the job but I'd be lying. You have a right to know. I'm not going to screw things up but I am seriously attracted to this woman. It took me by surprise. I…didn't expect any of this. Flat out, I just like her. After hearing the recording today, it seems pretty clear she's not involved with her uncle's operation. And she volunteers at a suicide hotline." He felt like a fool for letting his emotions get entangled but he wasn't a damn robot, and Lucy Carreras had gotten under his skin.

Colt let out a rough sigh. "This isn't the end of the world. Maybe it's a good thing. Because we might need to use her as an asset."

Leighton's jaw tightened. He didn't like the thought of using Lucy at all or even thinking of her as an asset. He understood this op was about more than him and his wants and needs, but that didn't mean he had to like it. Lucy was more than an asset.

"Are you going to be able to handle yourself?" Colt asked, continuing.

"Yes. She'll be working tonight and busy. I'll avoid her as much as possible as I scope the place."

"All right. Be careful though. I'm going to have Gage see if he can figure out who was tailing you. Maybe he'll pick up something on some CCTVs."

"Sounds good."

As soon as they disconnected, he turned off the water to the shower and scrubbed a hand over his face. He needed to get it together. Tonight he had to be on his game, to be Spencer Johnson, not Leighton Cannon.

Because Leighton had too much baggage.

* * *

"I'm second-guessing myself wondering if we should have pulled him," Colt said to Skye as they stepped into the barely lit kitchen of Michael Atkins's house.

At this point, they knew that the guy was likely missing—either of his own volition or not. He and Skye had sat on the guy's house for the last couple hours and hadn't seen any movement inside or out. No one else had approached the place. They'd checked his mailbox, and he hadn't checked his mail in the past eighteen hours.

Which could mean nothing at all. He could be lazy, but after he'd been fired all his credit cards and his cell phone had stopped all use. And he hadn't checked his email or social media.

It was the cell phone that made the team suspicious. Because the guy could just be lying low somewhere and paying cash. But not to use his cell or social media *at all?* Nah. Going on the guy's past cell phone record, the thing had been glued to him. He texted practically all day and night long.

So they were going to see if they could find the guy. Because one of two things had happened. He'd gone on the run because he was worried that one of Kuznetsov's men would kill him for being discovered by his niece— or he was already dead.

"I think Leighton's fine," Skye said, opening up Atkins's refrigerator. New, stainless steel, huge and filled with...beer. And nothing else.

"Why are you so sure?" Colt trusted her to be more objective than him because she hadn't known Leighton forever like him. And she was usually pragmatic about things regardless. His wife didn't put up with bullshit.

"He was honest about his feelings. He didn't try to hide anything from us. He was open about being attracted to her—and there was no reason for him to have told us other than to simply be straightforward. I trust that kind of honesty. And I trust him. He might have baggage but let's be real, we all do. I think he's got things under control."

"Always so wise," Colt murmured.

"This is true. I shouldn't have to keep reminding you." Though her back was turned to him, and she had on a ski mask, he could practically hear her grinning.

Shaking his head, Colt stepped onto a kitchen chair and started opening the higher cabinets. Atkins lived in a shotgun-style house that was long and narrow, in a more than decent neighborhood. They'd had to be careful about breaking in, and had been sure not to be seen by neighbors. Which always took some finessing. Nosy neighbors and dogs were often better security systems than cameras.

All the drapes were closed but there'd been a couple lights left on inside. So they hadn't touched anything. Gage hadn't been able to find a record of a security system and they hadn't seen one, but in case there were video cameras, they'd decided to completely cover themselves from head to toe. Ski masks, gloves, the whole works. They'd even put in contact lenses to change their eye color. This was definitely not their first rodeo.

"All this stuff is new," Skye muttered more to herself than him.

He'd noticed the same thing. All-new kitchen appliances and furniture, and a big-ass flat screen mounted on the living room wall above a fireplace that hadn't been used in ages. Everything was all shiny, though the place seemed mostly unused. Or maybe that was just because the guy was a bachelor. It wasn't dirty, but it wasn't neat and tidy either.

If there was one thing the Marine Corps had instilled in Colt, it was to keep his shit together and organized.

He snorted when he pulled out a box of Frosted Flakes and found a wad of cash rolled up in the bottom. Taking it out, he pocketed it.

"Stealing now?" Skye's tone was teasing.

"One of my lesser sins," Colt said. "We can add it to the fund for Maria." Because they *were* going to rescue her. Or at least he really hoped so. And there was no doubt she was going to need money to relocate with her mother and family—and that she'd likely need counseling. Considering her family wasn't swimming in wealth and had little or no health insurance, he figured they were going to need monetary help as well.

When the crew did jobs, they didn't do the bare minimum. Now wouldn't be any different.

"I like the way you think," she said, digging through Atkins's freezer. Then she let out a snort as she pulled out a bag of jewels. "Man, this guy is really not creative. He hides his shit in the most obvious places. Seriously, why not get a safe? Amateur," she muttered, shutting the freezer door and shoving the bag into her back pocket.

As she shut it, they both heard a loud knock on the front door, followed up with, "New Orleans Police, open up."

Oh hell. Atkins hadn't been reported missing. Or Colt wasn't aware that he had. He'd just been fired from his job in the early hours of yesterday morning. Technically he wouldn't be considered missing anyway. So why the hell were the cops here at one in the morning? Gage was on the comm with Leighton—who was at the casino right now—instead of them. Skye and Colt had decided to do this job solo since it had seemed easy.

They'd worked together a long time, even before they'd been married, so they didn't need to say a word as they fell in step together. It was time to run.

Moving soundlessly, they headed toward the back door even as there was another knock on the front door. Colt just barely slid one of the blinds covering the window in the back room and peered through the slit. There was a guy in uniform, a patrol officer, leaning against one of the fence posts, talking on his radio—not looking in their direction.

The cops were prepared...for something.

He looked at Skye. There was pretty much one choice at this point. Run. Good thing they were always prepared.

She nodded once as he put his hand on the back door.

"Open up or we're coming in, Atkins," the voice from the front shouted. "Now!"

Yeah, they needed to move. Colt opened the back door silently, looking out onto the back patio.

No matter how relaxed that cop was, he saw the movement as soon as Colt reached the edge of the porch.

Colt moved like hellhounds were after him, jumping off the porch and rushing the guy. He felt like a jackass for doing it but there was no way around it. Fist raised, he punched the guy even as the man started to reach for his weapon.

Skye was right with him, grabbing the Taser, then yanking the man's sidearm out and completely disarming him. It all happened so fast—though the guy got in a solid punch to Colt's ribs as he shouted, "Back here!"

Sucking in a breath, Colt took the pain as he slammed his fist against the guy's jaw.

The man dropped even as they heard shouts of alarm.

Neither he nor Skye responded. They simply sprinted across the backyard, putting distance between them and the fallen man.

"Stop and put your hands up! New Orleans Police!"

They didn't pause as they jumped over the back fence, racing through the neighbors' backyard.

He doubted the cops would be stupid enough to shoot at them in a residential neighborhood but they needed to disappear. Fast.

The key to getting away in a situation like this was disappearing in the first five minutes. Ten, tops. Because if law enforcement decided to put up roadblocks, it would be a hell of a lot harder to escape. Not impossible, and they'd escaped from worse situations in foreign countries. But it wasn't fun.

Heart pounding as they raced alongside the back neighbors' house, he and Skye made a sharp right as they hit the next block over.

They'd already had an adaptable escape plan in place so they knew exactly what they were going to do.

Timing was simply key. They needed to get to their getaway car before they were spotted.

Their shoes pounded against the sidewalk as they ran down the lamplit street. A couple walking their dog shouted in alarm as they raced by. Two people wearing ski masks and running was definitely not a good look. Two cars whizzed past, an SUV and a Jeep. Neither slowed.

As they reached the end of the street, he glanced back to see a man in a suit pursuing them. The guy had to be a detective and not a patrol officer. He digested all of that information in milliseconds as he and Skye rounded the corner, veering around a cluster of college-aged girls wearing tiaras, boas and beads in the middle of the sidewalk.

"Rude!" one of the girls shouted after them.

Yes! Their car was waiting where it should be. Skye palmed the keys and jumped into the front seat, starting the engine before he'd even made it into the passenger side. She gunned it, tearing away from their spot right as that cop rounded the corner and Colt slammed the door behind himself.

"He's on his radio," Colt said even as they sped away, putting more and more distance between them and the detective. "He'll get the plate."

"Too bad they'll be looking for the wrong vehicle," she said, glee in her voice.

He snorted softly as she took a hard right at the next stop sign. Moving swiftly, they jumped out of the crimson-colored muscle car and slid into their other backup vehicle. The real getaway car.

A four-door, gray sedan that was boring as fuck. The window tint was just dark enough that people could see movement inside but not anything important. Like faces.

"That's how you do a getaway right." Skye ripped off her ski mask as she pulled away from the curb.

He did the same, glancing behind them automatically, but no one was in pursuit. He could hear sirens in the distance, and maybe they were for him and Skye. But maybe not. New Orleans was a busy city.

They passed a Catholic church as she said, "Did you get a good look at our pursuer?"

"No. But he was a detective if I had to guess, only because he had on a suit." And as far as he knew, patrol officers wore uniforms.

Colt was just annoyed that he hadn't been able to get a better look at the guy. But he was sure that Gage could find out who had been at Atkins's house.

And more importantly, why.

CHAPTER EIGHT

—Dick-punching should be a sport.—

Leighton resisted the urge to look at his watch again as he sat at one of the bars. He knew exactly what time it was.

After one in the morning—and he was about to call it a night. He'd gambled and actually broken even tonight. Surprisingly. He hated everything about this place, especially since he wasn't drinking. At least a buzz might make the casino noise and scents tolerable.

He was acting as if he was drinking, but he was letting his drinks get watered down then switching them out for fresh ones before he was done. He needed to play his role of trust fund jackass who didn't mind blowing money and having a good time, but he sure as hell wasn't going to get drunk on a job.

It would be the height of stupidity to dull his senses. But it was getting late, and so far he hadn't seen anything or anyone that looked out of the ordinary. The whole team was scouring the city, following up on leads. Skye and Colt had already had one run-in with the cops barely half an hour ago so now they were outside the hotel sitting tight. Brooks and Nova were following around a smuggler in case anything interesting developed. And Savage and Axel were standing by on alert in case they were needed while Gage was doing scans of the security at the hotel.

"Got a hit," Gage abruptly said, his voice clear over the comm line.

"On what?"

"Maria Lopez."

Everything inside him stilled. "You're sure?" He barely moved his lips, kept his voice low so that no one around him could hear. The place was so loud anyway, the sound of slot machines dinging incessantly.

"Yep. About thirty feet from you. Behind the second row of slot machines closest to the lobby. Red dress. She looks different than the pictures but facial recognition says it's her. Eighty-eight percent."

This was it. Everything around him funneled out as he pushed away his watered-down vodka and tonic on the bar top and stepped away. As he did, he nearly collided with a beefy-looking security guy he'd seen around the hotel.

The guy barely glanced at him as he stepped up to the bar top and started talking to the bartender about an issue.

"Where's Lucy?" he murmured, making his way across the casino floor.

"Ah…don't have a hit on her. She fell off the radar about fifteen minutes ago. Stepped through a door marked 'Employees Only.' Not on any of the cameras."

Good. Leighton didn't want to run into her while this was going down. Because if this truly was Maria Lopez—

and he doubted Gage was wrong—he was getting her out of here no matter who got in his way.

As he made it to the slot machines, he nearly stopped in his tracks when he saw her. In profile, she was leaning up against one of the slot machines, dressed to the nines in a skintight red dress with sparkly gold jewelry and big gold hoops. Her hair was curled and her makeup done to make her look older than he knew she was. It was definitely Maria Lopez though.

His heart rate kicked into gear. "I'm getting her out now. I won't be coming back."

"Skye's already on the move," Gage said. "And the getaway car is ready."

Good. He'd wiped down his room every time he left it, but Skye would need to grab his stuff. Even if it was all basically disposable, he didn't want to leave a trace. As he neared Maria, he weighed his options as he covertly eavesdropped as she chatted up a man old enough to be her father. The guy didn't seem interested, however.

Yeah, he wasn't even going to be subtle. Not when getting her out quickly was key. Leighton moved in closer and smiled at her as he put money in the slot machine next to hers.

"Buy you a drink?" he asked.

She smiled at him but it didn't reach her eyes. Nodding, she turned away from the other man and stepped closer to him. "Rum and Coke would be perfect," she said, her voice slightly cracking.

He shifted their bodies slightly so that they were moving away from the man she'd been talking to. The cacophony of noise in this place never dimmed, so he doubted the guy could overhear them, but he was taking every precaution for her safety.

"Maria Lopez, your mother hired me to find you and get you out of here. Are you being watched?"

Her eyes widened slightly, hope flickering for a moment before the light dimmed. Her mother hadn't technically hired him but it was close enough to the truth. And he needed to get her out of here now.

"What's my mother's name?"

He rattled off her mother and father's names, and then gave the name of Hazel's grandmother, letting her know exactly how he'd been hired without revealing Hazel's name.

That hope was back. "My mother is safe?" she whispered. "You swear?"

"Yes. I promise. She left your father. Your sister is safe too."

"There are two men watching me that I know of. One works for security here and the other is dressed up as a guest. He's mean," she whispered. "And they're both armed and dangerous." Her shoulders sagged. "Just walk away now."

"I'm armed and dangerous too. And I'm not alone. You need to do exactly what I say, when I say, and don't question me. If you do, you'll get out of this alive and you'll be back with your family in no time."

"Okay." Her eyes glittered with tears but she quickly blinked them away, her jaw tightening with determination.

* * *

Lucy watched on the security feed as the man she'd kissed this afternoon walked off arm in arm with a woman who Lucy was fairly certain was an escort. She'd been watching the woman on the security feed for the last half hour as she approached various single men with what appeared to be clear purpose.

Lucy had been trying to figure out if the woman was with someone—or more accurately, if someone was forcing her to do this. Or if she'd just been working alone. But she hadn't been able to tell. No men had actually approached her, and no one who worked at the casino seemed to be paying attention to her.

Then, suddenly, Spencer had approached the woman as if on a mission. Lucy wasn't sure if she was feeling gutted because he'd kissed her only today—well, yesterday technically—and asked her on a date and was now clearly leaving with another woman, or if it was because he was leaving with a potentially exploited woman.

"What's wrong?" Nick asked as she headed out of the security room.

She'd just stopped by to check in with the team before she headed out for the night and had decided to check out the cameras. It was a freak accident she'd even seen Spencer because she hadn't been looking for him. While she trusted her uncle to investigate things—she knew Michael Atkins had been fired, so that was good—she still wasn't going to let this whole thing drop.

"Nothing," she said, smiling as she headed for the glass panel of doors. She wasn't even sure what she was going to do at this point. Confront Spencer? Maybe she was wrong and the woman wasn't an escort. Lucy wasn't sure if she was overreacting because she was attracted to Spencer. She'd never been jealous before. Not in a romantic capacity anyway. But her internal radar was pinging, and she wasn't going to ignore it.

It didn't take her long to make it to the first floor using the executive elevator. Weaving through people, she headed across the crowded lobby, but frowned when she saw Marco approaching Spencer and the woman.

Ugh. What was Marco doing here? Wait…did he know Spencer Johnson? Or the woman, maybe?

Ignoring one of the dealers who was motioning to her, she made a beeline for the two men and the woman.

Marco straightened when he noticed her. Spencer did the same, looking at her with an unreadable expression. Almost…blank. The girl was simply looking down at her stilettos, her olive complexion seeming overly pale under the lights.

Ignoring both men, Lucy focused on the girl. "Ma'am, are you okay?" The girl looked up at her and though her makeup was professionally done, she looked young and afraid. It was the fear in her eyes that knifed through Lucy. It was so raw and real. Something was definitely wrong.

"I'm fine," the girl whispered.

Lucy looked between Marco and Spencer, not sure what was going on. Spencer's hands were balled into fists, his jaw clenched tightly. Marco looked pissed too.

"Would you like to come with me?" Lucy asked the girl, once again ignoring the two men. She'd taken a few classes in college and knew to speak to potential victims directly. To let them know that you were there to help them.

"No, I don't want to go anywhere with you," the woman snapped before linking arms with Spencer. Marco made a step toward them as if to stop them, though Lucy wasn't sure why.

Without a word, Spencer started for the exit, the woman's heels clicking as they hurried away.

Marco started to go after them, but Lucy stepped in front of him. "What are you doing? How do you know that girl? How do you know Spencer?"

"You know that man?" he asked, ignoring her other questions.

"He's a high roller at the casino. We've given him some comps."

"I want his room number." Marco wasn't even looking at her, but over her shoulder at the retreating couple.

She snorted. "That would be a no. We value our guests' privacy. What is going on? Do you know that girl?" More importantly, was she okay?

Ignoring her, he muttered something under his breath as he glanced toward the exit again. Spencer and the woman were gone.

"I'll talk to you later," he ground out, completely dismissing her as he strode across the lobby.

Feeling at a loss for what to do, Lucy headed across the lobby as well. When she made it outside, she smiled at Reggie, one of the valet drivers.

He'd let his dark hair grow out. Tonight it was in a faux hawk. "Hey Lucy, how's it going?"

"Good," she said, scanning the line of cars for Spencer and the woman. "Did you see a man—white, about six feet tall with dark hair—come outside with a pretty Hispanic woman in a bright red dress?"

Reggie nodded, smiling. "Kinda hard to miss her. She was smokin'…ah, attractive." His cheeks flushed slightly. "They got into a waiting car."

"The car was already waiting for them?"

"Yep. A blue Altima."

She focused on Reggie now, since he'd really noticed the woman and remembered the car—which wasn't unusual for him. "Do you remember seeing her before?"

"Nope…and I would have."

"Okay, thanks." Feeling deflated, she headed back inside. She hadn't seen Marco again and she really didn't give a crap about him right now.

But she did want to find out more about that girl. If this Spencer Johnson was involved in trafficking or prostitution, she was going to bring him down. Inside, she radioed security and told Nick to meet her in the Presidential Suite. She didn't care about privacy at this point.

* * *

Lucy tapped her foot impatiently by the private elevators as she waited for Nick to join her. She should have just gone up to the Presidential Suite by herself but after she'd radioed him, he'd wanted to go with her. Which she understood. Maybe nothing wrong was going on, but her alarm bells were going off right now and she wasn't sure what to do with herself.

It was the fear she'd seen in the woman's eyes. So potent.

Marco refused to answer her phone calls, and everything about what had happened with Spencer was bothering her. The way he'd looked right through her, the way he'd left with that woman, who looked absolutely terrified, and there'd been a car already waiting for them. Not to mention the woman had clearly been targeting men at the casino before he'd approached her. Lucy couldn't help but think he was involved in prostitution.

At least they should have his information on file, because she was definitely going to the police. Well…if she had anything solid she would, because as of right now, there was nothing they could do. She knew that much. Her suspicions alone wouldn't let the cops do anything.

"Sorry," Nick said as he stepped up to join her by the elevator. "Your uncle told me a little bit about what you found last night. I wish you'd told me about it."

"Have you been able to get ahold of Marco?" she asked, ignoring what he'd said.

Nick shook his head. "I don't work for him and he has no reason to answer my calls."

She half-smiled at that. "I know. But something weird was going on with him and Mr. Johnson," she said. That was one thing she couldn't figure out.

The elevator doors opened in front of them so they both stepped in. She used her master passcode to take them to the correct floor. There were only a couple suites on this floor. As the doors opened, there was a woman carrying a small bag and staring at her cell phone, clearly engrossed in a loud game of Candy Crush. She barely glanced at Lucy and Nick as she stepped into the elevator.

Lucy murmured, "Excuse me" as she stepped past the woman.

She heard the door shut behind her as she and Nick moved toward the Presidential Suite doors.

"What are you hoping to find?" he asked.

"I honestly don't know. Everything about the situation was wrong, and I can't help but wonder if he's involved with whatever Atkins was involved in."

"We'll find out," Nick said.

Lucy lifted a shoulder. "The investigation will hopefully reveal that he wasn't working with anyone else who works here," she said as they reached the door.

Stepping inside the suite, she was surprised to find the lights on. The room looked perfectly neat as she strode inside, heading straight for the bedroom, because that was likely where any personal stuff would be. But she didn't find anything there. No bags, clothing, or personal items. No electronics or anything in the safe either. Nothing. All the toiletries provided by the hotel were neatly stacked in the bathroom, as if the room had never been used at all. The entire place was spotless. The only thing she could see missing was a couple apples from the complimentary fruit basket.

As she met Nick in the living room area, he frowned. "Are we sure this guy was even staying here? It looks as if the place hasn't been used. At least where I looked."

"The bedroom is the same."

"I can have someone sweep the room but I don't even know what you're looking for," he said.

She bit her bottom lip, feeling a little foolish. God, what if this was about nothing at all? What if Marco and Spencer had simply both been hitting on the woman…

No. Lucy wasn't going to second-guess her instinct. Not when the fear in the woman's eyes had been real. That's who she should be focusing on anyway. Maybe she could figure out who the woman was by doing a search on her image. She'd at least be able to find out if she was a guest, or had been in the past.

"I don't think it's necessary," she said. "I'm just hoping once we talk to Marco, maybe he'll be able to shed some light on whatever was going on."

"The guest probably isn't coming back."

"Yeah, I know," she said even as she received a radio call from the concierge informing her that Mr. Johnson had checked out via an online app. Of course he had.

Tonight just got weirder and weirder. "Come on," she said. "I'll head back with you to the security floor." Because she was going to at least try to see if she could figure out who the woman was.

"Okay..." Nick pulled out his own phone as he received a call.

She half listened to the conversation as they headed back to the elevators. "Is everything okay?" she asked as he ended the call.

"No. Some of our security feeds were corrupted."

That got her attention. "What do you mean?"

"I mean the security feeds from the hotel and some from the casino floor for the last hour were basically erased. There are other patches of time that seem to be missing too. It's like a virus was injected into them. The feeds are sent off-site but I don't like this at all."

She didn't like it either. Not one bit.

Now she wondered if this had something to do with Spencer. As long as she'd worked here, they'd never had an issue with security feeds or footage. And tonight of all nights, the last hour had suddenly been erased?

She was going to get to the bottom of why Spencer Johnson was here. It angered her that she'd actually gone out with him, let him kiss her. Worse, she'd liked it. A lot.

Maybe it wasn't prostitution at all, but someone was trying to rob them instead. It wouldn't be the first time someone had tried, and she knew it wouldn't be the last.

CHAPTER NINE

—You know what rhymes with Friday? Wine.—

"How are things looking?" Leighton asked Skye over the phone even as he glanced at Maria, who was silently crying. God, he wanted to kill Kuznetsov himself for how much pain he'd caused people. Savage was their getaway driver, but he'd been mostly silent since picking them up.

"Good," Skye said. "I ran into Lucy and some security guy on the way out but they didn't even pay attention to me. You think she'll be a problem for us?"

"I don't think so. I think she can be an asset." Leighton seriously hated using that word in relation to Lucy, but it was appropriate. "And I think I know how to bring her into this whole thing with us. Maria has told me that there are a lot more girls. She's been staying at a house fairly close to the hotel. She said they would drive her around for a while before going to the hotel, but it felt like they were driving in circles. She remembers what the house looks like at least and some markers nearby."

"Okay. Colt and I are headed back to the safe house."

"Good. I need to call Hazel."

"Gage already took care of it. He wanted to let her know so she could contact Maria's mother."

"Good." As far as Leighton knew, her mother and sister had relocated across state lines in a coastal Mississippi town after the mother had left her husband. It wasn't far, but Hazel was certain they'd be safe where they were. "I think we need to bring Lucy into this sooner rather than later. As in today." Leighton quickly outlined his plan to Skye, who was silent for a few moments after he finished.

"I think it's a good idea," she finally said. "Though it could backfire on us if she's involved with her uncle's organization."

"I know." Lucy could put targets on their backs if he was wrong about her. "But I don't think she is, and you don't either. When she approached Maria and me tonight, she looked right at Maria and asked her if she needed help." Her expression had been so fierce, and when she'd looked at him, all he'd seen was confusion and more than a hint of anger.

"Then I say we go for it. What happened with Broussard?"

"He tried to stop us on the way out. Started to threaten Lucy as we headed for the exit."

"Did he get a picture of you?"

"No."

"Okay, then. The room is cleared out with no evidence left behind that you were ever there. And Gage corrupted the security feeds, targeting any feeds that had you in them. So you should be in the clear. Oh, and Axel is currently at the place where the backup feeds go—he's breaking in tonight. Or this morning, actually."

They were definitely a well-oiled machine. "All this is good, but we can't be done. We need to save all these girls."

"Agreed. Do what you need to do with Lucy and then head back to the safe house. Do you think I should pick up Maria?"

He started to say no, but then changed his mind. "Yeah. Actually, why don't you meet us? Not Colt though. Too many people might spook Lucy when we tell her about…all this."

He disconnected and looked over at Maria, who had thankfully stopped crying. He'd given her a jacket earlier and she had it wrapped tightly around her. Soon he wanted to give her different clothes. It wouldn't erase anything that had been done to her, but he wanted to do whatever he could to make her comfortable.

"How do you feel about what I laid out?" he asked, because she'd heard the whole conversation between him and Skye.

She sniffed once. "I want to save those girls too. None of us were there by choice. It was the only reason they were able to keep us in line—almost all of us were afraid for our families. Those men were awful. This whole situation is awful. It shouldn't be happening, here of all places. Right under everyone's noses."

"I know. You really don't mind making a stop before we take you to your mom?"

"No. I heard everything you said."

"Okay." He looked at Savage in the rearview mirror. "You know where to go," he said to his friend.

Savage simply nodded once, his expression dark. He was just as angry about this whole thing as they all were. They definitely weren't going to stop with just helping one woman. Leighton wanted to burn the entire organization to the ground.

* * *

Lucy opened the door to her condo, then shut and locked it behind her before disarming her security system. She was exhausted and cranky. That being an understatement.

She'd tried calling her uncle and he hadn't answered, so she'd tried Marco again, but that jackass hadn't answered. The security team had been in a state of frenzy because someone had corrupted their files, and she absolutely understood why. But that wasn't her area of expertise so she'd let them do their thing. As far as they knew, no crime had been committed, the casino hadn't been robbed and their data seemed secure. Well, secure-ish, considering their feeds had been hacked. And Spencer Johnson hadn't done anything illegal. That they knew of anyway.

So she'd finally headed for home—and she'd never felt more useless in her entire life. If she thought it would do any good, she would call the cops. But she had no idea what to tell them at this point. That she suspected potential prostitution at the casino… So what? They would need proof.

Ugh. She needed sleep to clear her mind, and maybe once she was clearheaded, she'd figure out what to do. Heck, maybe her uncle would have called her back by then and he'd know what to do.

She slipped out of her heels and slid off her jacket, hanging it on the hook by the door before striding down the dark hallway. One of her motion-sensor night-lights flicked on as she moved past, illuminating her way. As she stepped into the kitchen she realized the lights were on—and she didn't remember leaving them on.

Less than a second later, she nearly let out a scream when she saw Spencer sitting there at her island countertop with the woman in the red dress. The woman was wearing a big jacket now and it looked as if she'd washed her face of all the makeup.

"How did you get in here?" Oh my God, who cared? *What* were they doing here? Preparing to make a break for it, she automatically tensed when Spencer held up his hands, palms outward.

"I hacked your security system then picked the lock. If I wanted to hurt you, I could have done it by now. So I hope you'll listen to what we have to say before you call the cops."

She nearly snorted. Because she had a feeling if he wanted to stop her, he could easily stop her from calling anyone. "I'm guessing your name is not Spencer." Not a question.

He shook his head. "No, it's not. I work with a group of people who help individuals in need."

Well that wasn't vague or anything.

The girl stepped forward slightly, her arms wrapped around her thin body. "My name is Maria. I've been held captive with many other women. We've been trafficked through various places around New Orleans, including The Sapphire." She held out an arm and pointed at Spencer—or whoever he was. For now, Lucy was going to think of him as Spencer. "This man saved me."

"How do I know you're not being held hostage by him right now?"

Taking her by surprise, Spencer pulled out a gun and set it on the island countertop.

Lucy had seen weapons before but she didn't like them at all. Icy fingers trailed down her spine, all the muscles in her body tensing. He could kill her right here, right now. There was nothing she could do to stop him.

Moving efficiently, he slid out the magazine, which she saw was full, then he popped it back in and handed it to the woman. "Safety's on." Then he stepped a few feet away, putting distance between himself and the woman. "If I'm holding her captive, would I give her a way to kill me?"

The woman laid her hand over the gun, but didn't do anything else with it. "He's not holding me captive. Like I told you, he saved my life."

Lucy rubbed her temple once. "Why not go to the police?"

She snorted. "They're not going to do anything. The man who traffics us, he's too powerful. And I'm pretty sure he has police in his pocket because..." Swallowing hard, she trailed off.

Lucy could fill in the blanks, however. Her stomach roiled. "So you freed her tonight?" she asked, turning back to Spencer.

"I did. It was a favor to a friend. We got a tip that The Sapphire was being used for trafficking. And I'm going to stop it. All of it."

"Okay. Let's say I believe you. If you can't go to the police, why not someone else? Like…the FBI, I guess?"

"It's complicated."

Lucy nearly jumped out of her skin when a woman with auburn hair stepped out from behind her like a ghost. It took a moment, but Lucy recognized her jawline. The hair had been a different color, but she recognized the woman who'd stepped onto the elevator playing Candy Crush. "Who are you?" she demanded.

The woman ignored her as she nodded at the woman in the dress. "Your mom is waiting."

"I'll answer any questions you want to know," the woman named Maria said, already moving away from the island countertop and that big gun still there. "But I need to go to my family. My mother is worried about me. And honestly, I'm exhausted. I wanted to tell you to your face that this man and his friends saved me, that I am grateful, and there's a serious problem in your hotel."

"What about the other man who was in the lobby?" Because Marco had to somehow be involved. Now Lucy had no doubt. And this changed everything she thought she knew.

The woman's face paled. "He is not a good man. He helps run all of us through the different hotels. And he doesn't stop there. He uses all of us. He rapes us. He is a very bad man. When he saw me leaving with him…" she said, motioning to Spencer, "he tried to stop us. He threatened my family, my little sister," she whispered, her voice cracking.

"I'm glad you're safe now," Lucy said, unsure what else to say.

Once the two women left, and only when she heard the door shut behind them did she turn toward Spencer. "What's your name?"

He sat back at the island, taking his gun and tucking it into a holster. For a long moment she thought he might not answer. Finally he said, "I'm Leighton. I'm sorry I had to lie to you. But the mission was to rescue Maria."

She didn't move any closer to him. Instead she remained in the entryway. "Your mission?"

He nodded once. "That's right. Saving her was the final objective."

Words like *mission* and *objective* sounded like law enforcement. "Are you in law enforcement or do you work for the government?"

"No. I'm going to be very upfront. The people I work with definitely work outside the law. And I'm not sorry. We don't have to worry about warrants or other bullshit when people are in danger. I'm here tonight because I think you're a good person. And I'm ninety-nine percent sure that you are not involved with trafficking those women."

She felt her temper rise. "Let's go with a hundred freaking percent. I'm not involved in any of that."

"Well, someone in your hotel is. More than just one person. And it could be more people than you imagined. And there's one thing for certain—your uncle is behind *all* of it. He runs a giant empire of criminal activity."

She let out a short, sharp laugh at this man's audacity. "You're full of shit. I told him what I suspected and he's opening an investigation."

The man in front of her, allegedly named Leighton, was the one who laughed now, though the sound was dry. "He's not opening an investigation. But he did kill Michael Atkins. I assume not personally but the guy is now dead. Likely on his orders."

She blinked once. "The security guy?"

"Yes. You can find that out on your own by making a few phone calls. His body was found less than an hour ago."

Lucy shook her head. "Why would he kill him?"

"A guess? Well, you discovered there was potential trafficking in The Sapphire. And Atkins was stupid enough to get caught by you. Since now it's pretty clear that your uncle has gone to a lot of trouble to make sure you're not aware of his operations, I'm going to guess that he's pissed Atkins got on your radar. I can't know for sure, but he's clearly tying up loose ends. But that doesn't mean this operation is going to stop. Obviously it's not after tonight."

He retrieved a folder from one of the chairs behind the island and laid it on the countertop.

"Here's some information I think you'll find interesting. It's a file on your uncle. You either believe it or you don't. If you want to help us stop the trafficking of women through The Sapphire, my contact information is in here. Or if you want to do nothing, then do nothing and be complicit." He pulled a little recorder out of his pocket and set it on the countertop. "This is a little extra for you. It's a recording of your uncle. Nothing that will put him in jail, but it's pretty damning." He shoved up and started to leave.

"Wait..." Her head felt as if it would explode right now with all this information overload. "Why..." Gah, what did she even want to ask? She should be shoving this stranger right out her door and calling the cops. "Why did you target me?" Because obviously that was what he'd been doing when he'd asked her out.

"Because you're related to a monster. But it's pretty clear you're nothing like him. For the record, however, I kissed you because I wanted to." He paused, those haunted eyes looking right at her, pinning her in place. "And I'm not sorry about it."

CHAPTER TEN

—Follow your own inner compass.—

L ucy jerked awake at the sound of her phone ringing. She'd finally dozed off after poring over the files Leighton had left for her. She wasn't sure how much of it was true but it certainly rang true. Some of the files were marked classified. And the recording she'd listened to? Her uncle had been talking to someone about "buying goods," and while the conversation had been vague enough that she understood it wouldn't hold up in court, it sounded shady. Like he'd been talking about buying...guns maybe. Or drugs.

While Leighton might not work for the government, he must know someone who did to have access to so much information.

When she saw her uncle's name on the screen she tensed, tempted not to answer it. But she had to, especially after last night. Trying to keep her voice as normal as possible, she said, "Hello."

"Lucy. How are you?"

"Okay. We had a rough night last night. Some of the security was compromised, which I'm sure you already know."

"I do. I've already been informed of the situation. We're taking measures to correct it."

She wondered what else he'd been informed about.

"I hear you had a run-in with Marco."

She sat up against her headboard and pulled her knees up to her chest. Sunlight filtered in through her bedroom window, bathing her blue and white comforter. "I did. And I'm a little confused about his behavior."

"He knew the man from last night. They've had issues in the past. He is not to be let back into our hotel. I've already alerted the front desk that he's to be added to our list of people to eject."

That sounded strange. "Okay. But why? I don't understand anything about last night." Which was pretty close to the truth.

"It's just personal stuff. Marco used to date the woman he was with. It's all bullshit," he said lightly. "But I don't want the man in my hotel or casino."

Yeah, that definitely sounded strange. And fake. Her uncle wouldn't care if Marco and some random guy had dated the same woman. That much she knew. He was definitely lying. "Okay. Fine with me."

"You said you knew him?" her uncle asked.

"About as well as any other guest. I did go out to lunch with him and show him some of the city. He said he was looking to buy real estate." She figured she'd better not lie about that. Because it wouldn't be that hard for her uncle to find out she'd gone out with "Mr. Johnson." She certainly hadn't kept it a secret. And right now, she wasn't sure anything in her life was true so she was going to be as honest as possible about everything she could. But she wasn't going to tell him that Leighton and the woman had been at her condo last night. Or about the information Leighton had left her.

"Okay, good. If he contacts you again, let me know."

She snorted. "I seriously doubt he'll bother contacting me. Do you think he could be involved with the security breach from last night?"

"It's definitely crossed my mind. We've got it under investigation."

"Have you heard anything new about Atkins, the guy we fired? Has he been working with anyone?"

"I don't believe so. Security hasn't closed the investigation yet but so far we just have evidence of him working alone. It seems as if he got some security codes from some employees who quit and was able to figure out which rooms weren't being used."

Lucy didn't buy that for a minute. They changed their codes often, and when someone was fired or let go they changed all the codes again. They cared about their guests' privacy. But she didn't want to push him now— she didn't want her uncle to suspect she knew he was lying. "Okay. Just keep me informed."

"I will. I'll be in town tonight. If you're free for dinner, I'd like to see you."

"Just let me know when and I'll be there." If she said anything else, it would definitely look weird.

Once they disconnected, she lay back against her pillow even though there was no way she could sleep. She'd barely got to sleep at all. Her mind had been running overtime.

114 | KATIE REUS

A stranger had walked into her life and dropped a bomb in it. And she didn't think he was lying. More than that, she didn't think the woman from last night had been lying. The fear and pain Lucy had seen in her eyes had been so real. She didn't think anyone could act that well. And why would they anyway? They hadn't asked Lucy for anything either. Not really. Leighton had said he wanted her help stopping trafficking and that...was pretty damn noble.

She scrubbed a hand over her face and picked up her personal cell phone instead of her work one. Then she called the number Leighton had given her.

He picked up on the first ring. "Yes?"

"I want to meet in person. But I don't think you should come back to my condo."

"I've got a place we can meet."

"Okay." She listened as he told her where to meet him. Lucy wasn't sure she trusted him, but at this point she had to talk to him, had to get more details.

Because something very wrong was going on at her uncle's hotel. And after what she'd seen and read in those files...she wasn't sure she knew what kind of man her uncle was at all.

* * *

"What do you think?" Leighton asked Gage, who was sitting across from him at the island countertop. They were the only two awake at this point. Leighton hadn't been able to sleep well after the interaction with Lucy, and Gage was a machine who seemed to never rest regardless.

"Well, she didn't mention anything about you or Maria to her uncle." Gage had heard the entire phone call since they'd hijacked her phone.

"Yeah, she was honest about going out with me but she didn't offer up any other information. And I get the feeling he was fishing."

Gage shook his head. "He must think she's stupid."

"I don't think it's that. He probably just doesn't expect her to question him. And he brushed her off with an easy story. A stupid one, that she could punch holes in if she wanted, but easy enough to explain away."

Nova stumbled into the kitchen, her dark hair pulled up in a bun. She half grunted at him but dropped a smacking kiss on Gage's face before stumbling to the coffee pot. "You guys are up early."

"No rest for the wicked," Gage murmured.

"I don't even understand what that means," she muttered. Then she sighed in happiness as she took her first sip of coffee.

"At least she agreed to meet with me," Leighton said. And Lucy hadn't pushed him on the location. Something that bothered him. He wasn't setting up a trap, but she didn't know that.

He'd hoped she would call last night. After he'd left her place, Leighton and the others had tried to figure out where Maria had been held based on the descriptions she'd given them. They hadn't had any luck but they were going to try again today. The city and roads here were confusing—and many were currently under construction. His GPS wasn't even fully correct here. It was a clusterfuck everywhere, and even with Gage's hacking skills they hadn't been able to retrace Maria's steps.

"Yeah, but I don't know that it's a good thing," Gage said. "She could be trying to set you up."

"You're meeting with Lucy today?" Nova asked as she sat down next to her fiancé, mug in hand.

"Yeah. She just called."

"I can go with you, and I think a woman should be there. I'm a more calming presence than Skye. She can be kind of intense. And this woman has just learned that a whole lot about her life is a lie. It probably wouldn't hurt to have another woman present."

Leighton looked at Gage.

"I swear to God you'd better not be asking Gage if it's okay for me to go," Nova muttered.

Leighton picked up his own coffee and kept his mouth shut.

"I'm going," she said, making the decision.

"Works for me," Leighton said.

Gage just frowned but didn't respond one way or another.

"I'm going to take a shower." Nova stood, yawning even as she picked up her mug. "Just let me know what the plan is."

"I'll be up in a couple minutes," Gage said. Once she was gone, he continued. "I need to show you something. I didn't include it in the file last night for Lucy because I don't know if we should tell her or not."

"What is it?" Leighton asked, surprised Gage hadn't told him about this before now—whatever this was. He always shared information with the crew.

"It's…" Instead of turning his laptop around, Gage got off his stool and strode to the breakfast nook by a panel of bay windows. He'd set a bunch of files on the table earlier. He grabbed one manila folder and came back to the island and set it in front of Leighton. "Read it. For the record, Hazel *knew* about this. And she didn't tell us. She didn't tell *you*. And I can't help but wonder why not."

Leighton flipped it open and started reading, his stomach coiling tight as he did. "Holy shit," he said. As he looked over everything, including a file that was most definitely classified, he glanced up at Gage. "How'd you get this?"

"I've got friends too."

If this was true… "So her uncle killed her parents and made it look like a murder/suicide?"

"It looks that way. There wasn't enough evidence to do anything about it years ago and he wasn't on the FBI's radar like he is now. He was someone they were keeping an eye on, and wanted to take down, but his empire wasn't like it is now."

"His own brother," Leighton muttered, still reading. Apparently Kuznetsov's brother had been planning to testify against him for murdering a local store owner who wouldn't pay protection money. Lucy's father hadn't been squeaky clean, but he hadn't been a lowlife either. From this file, it appeared as if he didn't mind taking stuff that "fell off a truck" but he wasn't a murderer.

The man who'd been murdered had been a father of two young girls. That was what had pushed him to go to the Feds. And it had gotten him killed.

"Yep. Her father was going to turn evidence against him. Kuznetsov must have had his own contact within the FBI because he killed his brother before he could do anything."

"Jesus. This will hurt her." That being an understatement.

"Honestly, I don't know if we should tell her. I think you should make the decision because you're the one who's interacted with her."

Hell. Leighton didn't want to make that kind of decision. Even if it would fully bring her over to their side, he didn't know if it was necessary. For some reason, he found he cared very much about Lucy's feelings. He didn't want to hurt her at all. "Is this guy retired? The one who gave you all this?"

"Yeah. This never sat well with him either. He considers Kuznetsov his 'white whale' case."

"You sure Hazel knew about this?" Leighton couldn't understand why she wouldn't have told him.

"I honestly don't know how she couldn't have known."

Leighton tucked the information away, planning to call Hazel after he'd met with Lucy. Now he needed to grab a shower himself and head over to the meet point. He ignored the way his heart rate kicked up at the thought of seeing sweet, curvy, sensual Lucy.

CHAPTER ELEVEN

—We've got your six.—

L ucy second-guessed herself for the hundredth time. So maybe she wasn't certain she should be here meeting with a man who was a virtual stranger—a man who'd clearly somehow bypassed the casino security system. And the security system of her condo, which definitely hadn't helped her sleep any last night.

Either he'd bypassed the system to rob the casino, which so far didn't seem to be the case, or he'd done it to erase all footage of himself there. Because apparently all footage of him there *had* disappeared, according to security.

She found out that little nugget of information from Nathan—who'd heard the security guys talking—a couple hours ago.

Which made all of this that much weirder. But if Leighton wanted to hurt her, he could have easily. More than once.

Hell, maybe he'd still try but she was at least coming prepared. She'd opted to wear jeans, a sweater and sneakers today instead of her normal heels. She'd tucked pepper spray into her back pocket and strapped a knife to her ankle.

The knife had actually been a gift from her uncle, of all people. As well as the ankle strap. She'd never carried it anywhere, but today she was making an exception.

Obviously she hoped it didn't come to that. She hoped... She wasn't sure what she hoped at this point. Maybe just for answers.

As she reached the top step of the double-gallery house, the door swung open and a pretty woman with long brunette hair smiled at her. She'd been expecting Leighton, and for some reason this threw her off guard.

"I'm Nova. I work with Leighton. And I know you're Lucy. Please come in."

Frowning, she stepped inside with the pretty woman. Leighton and another man were off to the right, sitting at a long, formal table in an ornately decorated dining room. She wondered if they were the only three people in this house. And she wondered who the other two were.

"Like I said, I work with Leighton, and this is Gage, my fiancé." Nova motioned to the other man who looked as grim as Leighton.

Both men nodded at her and remained leaning against the dining room table.

She wasn't sure what to do now. Wasn't sure about anything. She was the one who'd wanted to meet with him and now she felt like she was drowning.

"Before we go any further, we're going to have to scan you," the one named Gage said.

She blinked. "Wait...what?"

"We've got to scan you for electronics."

She could actually understand why they were doing that but it didn't negate that it made her feel vulnerable as she held her arms out. She was grateful when Nova started scanning her with a wand and felt more at ease when the woman shot her an apologetic look. The woman could be lying, merely acting for Lucy's benefit, but it still made her feel better. Nova found her knife and pepper spray but didn't attempt to take them.

"Smart," was all she said.

When Nova was done, Lucy shoved her hands in her front pockets. Without her heels on she felt more vulnerable, as if she was missing part of her armor. "I read over the files you gave me. You could have doctored them."

"We could have," Leighton said. "But you must know that we didn't. Otherwise you wouldn't be here. You're too smart."

"I don't know about how smart I am. Because if what's in those files is true, I was raised by a monster and didn't realize it." The recording itself hadn't been monstrous, but the files indicated he sold people, drugs and guns, used charities as covers for his schemes, strong-armed people out of their own businesses because he wanted to purchase them for himself—at a heavy discount. And the list went on. Maybe that was the reason Liliana had been targeted for kidnapping in the past.

"He's gone to a lot of trouble to create a public persona for himself," Gage said as Nova sat down at the table.

The men followed suit so Lucy stepped into the room fully and sat down on the other side of the table from them. On the side closest to the door. She might not be able to take them on, but she could run fast if necessary.

"Is the woman from last night safe?"

"Yes," Leighton said, his haunted eyes still sad even as he watched her like a lethal predator. Damn it, she should not be noticing anything about him. "But there are more women being held. We plan to save them."

"How?"

The three of them looked at each other but didn't respond. *Fine.*

"What do you want from me?" she tried.

"Nothing," Leighton said. "Other than for you not to tell your uncle about us."

She rubbed her temple once. At this point, she wasn't telling her uncle anything. She didn't trust him. "Is Marco Broussard really involved in trafficking women?"

"Oh there's no doubt of that," Gage said.

"I guess I still don't understand why you guys haven't gone to law enforcement. Because it's clear you have access to classified documents." She was going to go on the assumption the papers he'd given her were real. They certainly looked real. Some of the stuff… It rang so true she had to believe it. Especially the recording where he talked about moving "product" through a charity. His words had been so vague and not legally damning, but a freaking toddler would be able to understand the double meaning.

"Things with law enforcement are complicated right now. Rescuing some trafficked women isn't high on their priority." Nova's tone made it clear she was frustrated. "The Feds are looking to bring down your uncle," she said. "He's their priority, not saving some random women."

Gage cursed next to her, and Leighton's jaw simply tightened.

Nova lifted a shoulder, clearly not concerned. "What? If we're going to bring her into this we need to be honest. Like I was saying," Nova continued, looking at her. "They want to bring him down. For good. But they want to bring him down for something a hell of a lot bigger. They want to make sure he *never* gets out of jail. And there's not enough tying him to the trafficked women. It's small potatoes for the Feds and even though I hate to say it, they can be assholes."

"So you have contacts with the FBI?"

"Yes," Nova said. "It's how we found out about the girls in the first place."

"You said that Maria was your operation. Your...objective?" Lucy looked over at Leighton.

He simply nodded but offered no more information, which was just frustrating as hell.

"Okay, so you're not going to tell me why. Fine. Now that your *objective* is over, you want to rescue the rest of these women? These alleged women?"

"You know there is no 'alleged' to it."

After the video feeds she'd seen at the casino, and after the phone call she'd made to a detective friend—a man she'd gone on a couple dates with—she'd found out that Mike Atkins was indeed dead. Not just dead, but murdered. So yeah, something very strange was going on.

"So why can't you rescue them?"

"Because we don't know where they are." Frustration laced Leighton's voice and was mirrored in Nova and Gage's faces.

"Why not put a tracker or like a GPS or...whatever on Marco? Because I'm pretty sure you're the one who hacked our casino—"

The one named Gage cleared his throat. "That was me, thank you very much. I hacked the casino feeds and disabled your apartment's security system."

Leighton simply snorted, though his lips curved up in a half-smile that made her think things she had no business thinking right about now.

"So...you hacked the casino's security. Which takes a whole lot of skill." She knew how many security measures they implemented. "Without really knowing more about what you guys do, I still have to assume you could somehow track him, right? Like with his phone or something? You knew where I lived. And you broke in." Which was something she wasn't going to think about.

"He's careful. Everyone is careful. I can track the phones of pretty much any employee your uncle has but my guess is that they must go dark when they transport the women. They must leave all electronics when they move them. Or they use burners. My guess is Broussard uses a burner phone because the phone registered in his name sits at his house pretty much 24/7."

"How can I help?" she asked even though she should not be getting involved with these people. But how could she not? How could she sit back and do nothing?

"We don't need any help," Leighton said, even as Gage straightened slightly.

"What we need is to figure out the location of where Broussard spends most of his days," Gage said. "Because I think he'll lead us back to those women." Gage glanced once at Nova before continuing. "We spoke to Maria last night and he's almost always at the house where they're being held. He leaves for short periods of times but always comes back. And not using a driver. We've only ever seen him with a driver, so he must have a vehicle he's using."

"He drives an Audi."

They all looked at each other.

"What?" Lucy asked.

Gage frowned. "You're sure?"

"Sure enough. He always drives one when he's at my uncle's house. I don't know what he drives around though. I've just seen him in an Audi more than once. It's black. Maybe I could plant something on his car."

Gage started to respond when Leighton shot him a sharp look, his jaw tight. "She's not going to plant a tracker on anyone. That's bullshit. It's too dangerous for her to get that close to him."

"If what you're telling me is true, then I'm going to help." And she wasn't asking.

Now Leighton turned and frowned at her. At her! He was the one who'd inadvertently dragged her into all this.

"My uncle gets into town tonight. I'm supposed to meet him for dinner. There's a good chance Marco will be there."

"I don't like this," Leighton said, shoving up from the table.

"Well, I don't like a lot of this," she snapped out. "So I guess it's a good thing I didn't ask for your opinion."

Nova snickered, then covered the laugh with a fake cough.

Under other circumstances Lucy might have laughed too. But she'd found out that her entire life was a giant lie. Okay, maybe not all of it, but right now she was trying to come to terms with everything new she'd learned. What if these people were lying to her?

"Look, you're not planting a tracker on anyone," Leighton said, even as Gage nodded. "Now that we know what he's driving, we'll just track him. It must not be registered in his name."

"Fine, but I still want to help."

"The information about his car is a big help," Leighton said, rounding the table. He respected her personal space even though it looked as if he wanted to step closer.

"Your uncle is really going to be here tonight?" Gage interrupted, drawing her attention to him.

She nodded once.

The three of them exchanged a glance, making her frown. "What?"

"The Feds want to bring him down," Nova blurted out. "And there are a bunch of them here. In New Orleans. If he's coming here, there's a good chance they might try to arrest him here if they're able."

"And if he gets wind of it," Leighton said, throwing a sharp glance at his friends, "he could cut his losses and run. He would dispose of any evidence that could bring him down."

He emphasized the word *evidence* and it took Lucy a long moment to register what he meant. Though she wasn't sure she completely understood. "Wait...are you saying he'd kill the women?"

"Yes," Leighton said simply. "They're not people to him. He probably wouldn't do it himself, but if the Feds come after him, his men will have orders to go scorched earth on anything tied to him."

She knew what she'd read in those files, and knew there was a lot of suspicion on her uncle that he'd committed a lot of crimes, including running drugs and people. Weapons too, though he seemed not to do much of that. Not to mention money laundering. So she wasn't sure why she was surprised about murder. She wasn't surprised, it just... She was having a hard time wrapping her head around everything. She wasn't sure she'd ever be able to come to terms with it. But if he was guilty, he deserved to go to jail. To pay for his crimes.

"If you're meeting your uncle tonight," Gage continued—and she was glad, because she couldn't find her voice— "I think we should put something on you. It's doubtful that your uncle will hurt you, but it wouldn't hurt to be prepared. Unless he has you checked when you visit?"

"He doesn't. I'll take a tracker." And she wasn't going to second-guess her decision. That woman had been afraid of Marco last night. God, had it only been last night? It seemed like an eternity had passed since then. Lucy could admit she was afraid of her uncle at this point. She would take the small backup being offered.

CHAPTER TWELVE

—Your instinct is your best friend.—

L eighton locked the door behind Lucy as she left, re-
sisting the urge to follow after her. He didn't like any
of this. He didn't want her involved in any of this. And it
was his fault she was. If she'd never seen him leaving the
hotel with Maria, he might have been able to salvage
something between them. Made sure she stayed far away
from all this.

"She's a smart cookie," Skye said, coming down the
stairs. The entire crew was at this house. It wasn't their
safe house but another one they'd rented as a backup not
far from where they were all staying.

He turned around to face her. "I know. But that
doesn't mean I have to like her going into danger."

"She's just having dinner with her uncle. One that was
planned. Besides, we'll have her back."

He nodded once, not exactly mollified but feeling
slightly better. Under normal circumstances, one of
them would have tried to infiltrate Kuznetsov's New Orleans home or Marco's and plant a tracker themselves.
But Kuznetsov knew some of their faces, and if he figured out Brooks was involved in this, it put all of them
in danger.

The way Leighton felt about Lucy was confusing as hell. "I need to make a phone call," he said abruptly, heading up the stairs. He needed privacy to make this call.

He called Hazel using FaceTime instead of a simple phone call because he wanted to see Hazel's face when he asked her what he needed to. He'd known her for a long time and there was something to be said for witnessing a physical reaction.

Hazel answered on the third ring. "Hey," she said, half-smiling at him. She looked exhausted, her short hair pulled back in a little tail. She had on a plain blue T-shirt and her badge was hooked around her neck on a chain.

"You working right now?"

"I'm always working. Until we close this case I'm basically not sleeping. Thank you again for saving Maria."

"Is she okay?" he asked.

"I think she will be. As soon as this shit is done, I'm going to figure out some things for them, but they're okay where they are now."

"Let me know if you need help in that area." Because the crew would have no problem relocating her. Though if Kuznetsov was taken down, it might not matter. They might be able to go back to their lives.

She smiled again and shook her head. "Look, is this important? Because if not, I really do have a lot of work to do."

"Are you guys close to bringing him down?" He didn't need to specify who.

She simply nodded.

"As in the next day or two?"

She nodded again.

"Did you know that he killed Lucy's parents?" he asked bluntly.

Surprise at the question flickered in Hazel's eyes even as a teeny bit of guilt bled through. "Where did you hear that?"

"That's not an answer. You're deflecting. So I'll take that as a yes." Annoyance sparked inside him.

She rubbed a hand over her face, sighed. "You didn't need to know."

"I think I get to decide what I need and what I don't need, especially when I'm doing you a favor."

"What does it matter? I needed you to save Maria and you did. His niece's background isn't important."

Well it was important to Leighton. "You know she's not dirty, right? She's not like her uncle." Not even close.

"I do know that. But I also know that sometimes innocent people get caught in the crossfire."

"What the hell does that mean?"

She lifted a shoulder and rubbed a hand over her face again. When she did, the phone moved slightly and he realized she must be in a hotel room. He knew the Bureau had put the agents up somewhere but she hadn't been able to tell him where because of security protocols. Though if he wanted to find out, he was certain Gage could figure it out.

"I'm just saying that if we can't get everything we need, there's been talk about putting pressure on her to bring her uncle down."

And telling her that Kuznetsov was the one who killed her parents would be the leverage the Feds needed to turn her. Yeah, Leighton definitely didn't like the sound of that. But he wasn't going to show any of his cards now. He simply nodded. Hazel had confirmed what he needed to know about Lucy's parents. "Good luck bringing him down."

"Thanks," she said with that half-smile again. "I'll talk to you later."

When he was done, he headed back downstairs to find everybody gathered in the dining room. Soon they'd leave, but in shifts to make sure they weren't followed. "I just got off the phone with Hazel," he said. "She confirmed that Kuznetsov killed Lucy's parents. I don't have any details other than what's in the file Gage's friend gave him. She also said that there's been talk of using Lucy to bring her uncle down. Putting pressure on her if necessary."

That got a whole lot of frowns from the crew. They knew how the Feds worked and didn't like it any more than he did.

"If it comes down to it I want to make sure we're all on the same page. We need to be her backup. If she needs an attorney or she needs us to blackmail someone into getting them to back off, I'm going to do it." And he definitely wasn't asking for permission. They'd gotten a ton of blackmail-worthy information from a job a while ago—one that inadvertently involved Kuznetsov himself.

"Agreed," Skye said before anybody else could talk. "I like her. She could've just pretended all of this shit wasn't real then gone back to her life. Instead she's aware and horrified by her uncle."

Everyone else nodded in agreement.

Not that he really expected less, but he felt oddly protective of Lucy and he was going to do everything to make sure she came out of this okay.

* * *

Lucy had never been more nervous in her entire life than she was now. Even though she'd sworn she wouldn't second-guess herself, as she stepped into the six-car garage at her uncle's New Orleans home, she wondered if she was making a mistake. What if she got caught?

No. The little voice in her head told her to shut up and just do this. Ugh, when had her life gotten so complicated?

And why couldn't she stop thinking about Leighton? She shouldn't be attracted to him. She shouldn't be thinking about him at all other than in terms of what she was doing here. Instead she found herself ridiculously attracted to him, fantasizing about him and his big, callused hands. Which told her she was seriously messed up in the head. Clearly she had damage.

Marco always parked his car in the garage when he was here, so she was peeking inside to see if it was there. God, she loathed the man. She shouldn't be doing this, shouldn't even be contemplating it. But maybe it would help Leighton and his people to find Marco faster. So...she was going to plant the tracker they'd put on her, on Marco's car.

Leighton would probably get all sexy and surly looking if he knew what she was doing.

Stop thinking about him. It wasn't as if there were security cameras inside the garage. On the outside of it, yes, but not in here. She knew, because she'd been in the small security room before.

Sure enough, Marco's car was in the garage, which very likely meant he was here. Gage and Leighton had said that he took a driver everywhere and maybe that was true. But she'd only ever seen him drive the Audi to her uncle's place. Of course, her interactions with him were few and far between, thankfully. Whenever her uncle was in town, he was so busy with him, she rarely saw Marco, and only here.

Before she could question herself again, she took the tracker out of her purse and hurried across the garage.

With damp palms, Lucy fastened it to the underside of one of the wheel wells. Moving quickly, she hurried back across the garage, hoping to be basically invisible until she found her uncle. Her heart was a wild, staccato beat in her chest, but she'd done it. Now she just needed to tell Leighton.

As she swung the door open, she bit back a gasp as she nearly ran into Gervasi, one of her uncle's employees. He was big, Russian and intimidating.

"What are you doing?" He frowned, sweeping her from head to toe in an assessing gaze.

She returned his frown with one of her own, making sure she played the haughty niece to perfection. "Excuse me? Am I not allowed in my uncle's garage?"

His eyes widened slightly and he took a step back. "No, no. That's not what I meant."

She smiled politely and passed him, dismissing him with an annoyed little sniff even though that wasn't remotely her personality. Her heart pounded wildly as she walked away from him. She'd taken a risk tonight and hoped it paid off.

Fear bloomed deep inside her chest as she wondered what would happen if Marco found the tracker. Or what if her uncle found out she'd placed it on Marco's vehicle? All questions she couldn't answer. Not to mention that not many people had access to this garage and now there was a witness who'd seen her leaving it. Damn it, maybe she should have thought this through more.

Heart pounding, she forced a smile as she stepped into the kitchen. Her uncle was where he'd told her he'd be. He hadn't wanted to eat in the formal dining room, but at the center island in the expansive kitchen instead. Which was fine with her.

She smiled brightly and crossed the tile to him, her heels clicking loudly. She kissed him on both cheeks as he smiled down at her, his pale blue eyes unreadable. His blond hair was cut short like usual and he wore a custom-made suit. Just like usual. He seemed normal enough.

"You're looking well," he said, the faintest hint of an accent in his voice. He'd worked very hard to lose that accent when it pleased him.

Her father had been the same way, though he'd never lost it. Her mother, a Cuban immigrant, had never lost hers either. Lucy shut the lid on thoughts of her parents right now, however.

"I should, I utilize the spa at the hotel any chance I get," she said teasingly.

He glanced over at his personal chef. "You may leave us now," he said flatly. His tone was so different than the one he used with her or with his daughter. There was no warmth, no civility even. With his son he was nominally warmer, but not by much.

In fact, she realized that he was only ever gentle with her or Liliana. She wondered so many things about him now. If the files she'd read were true. Her stomach was twisted up inside but she was going to force herself to eat tonight no matter what.

"Would you like a glass of wine?" He headed over to the crawfish étouffée and rice the chef had prepared where a bottle of Beaujolais waited.

"I would like a glass but since I'm driving, I'll pass tonight." She was already jittery enough, she didn't need to add alcohol to her system.

But he waved his hand once in the air. "One will be fine." And that was that.

When he made his mind up about something, it was always seen as settled. She'd never really pushed back either.

"You'll be happy to know that the investigation has been officially closed." Her uncle pulled down two bowls from one of the cabinets and started scooping out the étouffée onto rice.

"It is?" That seemed fast.

"Yes. Atkins was working alone. Thought he could make some extra cash on the side." Her uncle shook his head as if disgusted by the idea. "He is a fool. And he will never work in this town again. Not that it matters. It seems he has left town," he added on.

Lucy knew that was untrue and there was no reason for her uncle to lie to her—unless he was covering something up. "Good. I hate the idea of something like that in our hotel. It's disgusting," she added, watching to see if he reacted at all.

But he didn't. Instead, he served food into the bowls and motioned for her to sit at the island. "Sit, sit. I know you've been working hard."

"No harder than you," she said in what she hoped was a teasing manner but her movements felt stiff and brittle. If he noticed, he didn't let on.

She forced herself to take a deep breath. She could do this. Her uncle wasn't going to hurt her regardless. Right? A week ago she would have known the answer to that, but now she wasn't sure of anything.

"We've also figured out the issue with the security system. It's just a glitch, something that should have been fixed during the last security update."

"Seriously?" She took the wine glass he held out for her. Even if she didn't want any alcohol in her system, the red wine was honey smooth.

"Yes. And I've already fired the IT people who should have caught this issue before now. So there should be no more issues."

"Good."

"So, Marco seems to think you know that Mr. Johnson more than you let on. Is there something I should know?"

"Marco knows nothing," she snapped out. "I don't understand why you let him run all over The Sapphire. He's annoying."

Her uncle lifted an eyebrow in true surprise. Probably because she'd never let on how much Marco's presence bothered her. "You don't care for him?"

She lifted a shoulder. "Not really. He's bossy, arrogant and he gets in my way. He talks to me as if I'm missing brain cells." And the fool liked to call her princess on occasion.

Her uncle reached out and patted her hand once. The gesture felt condescending. "He means well."

The hell he did. Instead of returning to the topic of Marco, she said, "So have you thought more about Christmas?" Lucy knew this was the only topic guaranteed to take her uncle's mind off Marco and "Spencer Johnson."

His mouth pulled into a thin line as he speared a piece of salmon with his fork. "I thought this topic was closed."

"No. It's not. Liliana wants to come home for Christmas. Or to stay with me. And I'm not going to tell my cousin that she can't be here for the holidays. A cousin who is more like a sister to me."

"We'll see, we'll see."

She knew exactly what his "we'll see" meant but at this point she was just making conversation to keep him distracted from other topics she most definitely didn't want to talk about.

As soon as she left, she needed to call Leighton and tell him she'd placed the tracker. He might be mad at first, but what was done, was done. She wasn't sure if it would do any good, but seeing Marco's vehicle in the garage told her that he was definitely here. And he was staying out of sight, clearly. Because normally he always came around whenever she was with her uncle. So he must be avoiding her. Maybe she was reaching, but her instinct told her that he was likely avoiding her after the other night.

·

CHAPTER THIRTEEN

—You were not supposed to happen.—

Lucy leaned back against her front door and shoved out a breath. Tonight had gone...well, she wasn't sure. Things had seemed normal enough with her uncle, but she was second-guessing everything. Especially since she'd made the decision to plant that tracker.

Groaning to herself, she slipped off her bright red Manolos before she hung her coat by the door. She'd texted Leighton, simply telling him that she'd planted the tracker on Marco's vehicle. He hadn't responded and now she wasn't sure if she should call him or what.

When she stepped into her kitchen, she nearly yelped to find Leighton sitting there all cool as ice.

"Sorry," he murmured, standing. And he actually did look apologetic.

"What are you doing?" She didn't hang back this time. She wasn't afraid of him. Maybe she should be, but...she was going with her instinct on this. Of course, her instinct hadn't set off any alarm bells where her uncle was concerned, so maybe she should get that checked.

"I got your text. I was worried."

Rolling her eyes, she headed over to her refrigerator and grabbed a bottle of water. "Well don't be. I'm not going to tell my uncle anything."

142 | KATIE REUS

"I meant I was worried about you." His expression was so sincere, those haunted eyes watching her carefully. "What you did was dangerous."

"Oh." She fiddled with the bottle, not sure what to say. "I thought you might be angry about it."

"I am. I hate that you put yourself in danger like that."

Oh. She bit her bottom lip, not sure how to respond to his honesty.

"How did things go with your uncle?" he asked and some of the tension in her shoulders loosened.

"Okay, I think. I...I second-guessed my decision to plant it on Marco's car," she admitted, stepping closer to the island. She set the bottle down as she leaned against it. Nerves still rattled through her, making her edgy.

Leighton let out a low curse and stepped closer. Then he paused and grabbed one of the high-back chairs. "Sit."

For some reason it didn't sound like an order, but more like a request. Gratefully, she took the seat and was glad when he sat too. The man was so tall it was easier to talk to him when they were more at each other's level.

"Did anyone see you?"

"No. Maybe."

His entire body tensed as he went into what she thought of as *predator mode.* "Maybe?"

"Yeah." Lucy quickly relayed what had happened and didn't pull back when he took her hands in his as if it was the most natural thing in the world.

"I don't like that."

"Well, what's done is done. My uncle pushed me a little on 'Spencer' but mostly left it alone. We talked about family stuff mostly."

"Family stuff?"

She nodded, but didn't mention Liliana. She would never do that.

"Like his daughter?"

She froze. "Excuse me?"

"We know he has a daughter. And we'd never hurt a child. Ever. He's the monster, but that doesn't mean his family should pay for anything he's done. He deserves to go to jail for what he's done though."

She nodded, thinking of one of the files she'd read. "He really does."

"I'm sorry you're in this position. I'm sorry…I dragged you into this." Leighton cupped her face and gently wiped her cheek.

And she realized a few tears had spilled over. Jeez, she hadn't even known she was crying. All this was too much to deal with, however.

Then, suddenly, his mouth was on hers, sweet and teasing.

Oh, no. This was not good.

She leaned into him, surprised at the minty flavor as his tongue teased against hers. Heat bloomed inside her as his hand slid back, cupping her head now.

What was she doing? What was *he* doing?

She jerked back suddenly and he let her, though he was breathing as hard as she was. "You don't need to seduce me," she muttered, angry at herself for getting caught up in the moment.

He blinked, confused. "What?"

"I've already planted the tracker and I'm not saying anything to anyone."

"I kissed you because I wanted to. Even though I know I shouldn't. I kissed you because it's all I've thought about since I met you—even when I thought you were a criminal like your uncle."

Oh. Well, then. She nervously bit her bottom lip and was surprised when his gaze landed on it.

He let out a low groaning sound. "I really want to make you come."

She jolted at his boldness. "Did you just say that?"

He did that groaning, growling thing again as his gaze landed on her mouth. Again. "Yep. I want to taste your pussy—"

She grabbed his shirt, pulling his face to hers only to shut him up. Okay, it was to kiss him senseless. She'd never been with anyone into dirty talk and she really liked it. Even if it made her feel inexperienced and out of sorts.

He took over immediately, shifting slightly so that he was standing between her legs even as he continued kissing her. Or dominating her mouth was more like it.

He wrapped her up in his arms, holding her close as he teased her tongue with his, learning what she liked. She moaned into his mouth, her breathing growing harsher when he slid a hand down her back, cupping her butt.

When he said he wanted to taste her, he didn't mean right now. Did he? Even the thought of him going down on her, of seeing his dark head between her legs, got her more than hot and bothered. Heat detonated inside her, warmth flooding between her legs as she squirmed against him.

He pulled back slightly, nipped at her jaw. Her nipples beaded tightly as he nipped again.

"Where'd you go right now?" he asked.

"Hmm?" She wasn't quite beyond talking, but she was getting there. She didn't want to talk right now. And she definitely didn't want to think. Because then she'd get all caught up in her head. Then she'd start doubting herself and right now she really, really wanted to just feel. To experience whatever was going to happen with Leighton.

"Something got you turned on," he murmured, nipping at her earlobe now. "Something more than just my kisses."

"God, you're a talker," she murmured, making him laugh.

He pulled back slightly, watching her intently. It was seriously unnerving, especially because she could imagine him watching her like this while he was thrusting inside her. Oh God, that thought made her squirm too.

"You just went somewhere else again. What are you thinking?"

"Nothing."

146 | KATIE REUS

He simply lifted an eyebrow and went back to nibbling along her jaw. She dug her fingers into his shoulders, arching into him as he lifted her up onto the countertop.

"If you won't tell me, I'll just have to guess what you want." His words were as sensuous as the hungry look in his eyes. He started to push her skirt up, but paused. "May I?"

She should say no, but she really, really wanted to let this go wherever it was going to. Would she regret this later? Maybe. But she'd never know if she didn't let go. "Yes." The word was a whisper, but there was no hesitation.

"We stop if you say stop." Then he leaned forward at the same time she did, teasing her with that wicked tongue as he pushed her skirt up and over her hips.

The countertop was cool against her butt, making her shiver. When he reached for the flimsy material of her thong, she shivered again.

He barely took his mouth off hers as he pushed it down and off, tossing it to the side. Still kissing her, he cupped her mound gently, not penetrating.

Everything about this moment was exhilarating. It felt weird and seriously hot to be half dressed with him holding her like this. Her nipples were tight points against her bra cups, oversensitized more than they'd ever been. All her muscles were pulled tight as they kissed, as she waited for...something more.

Something like him sliding that thick, callused finger inside her. When he did just that, she moaned into his mouth. He felt so good and she was so wet.

She could admit that she was nervous and questioning her decision right now. But not enough to stop. Nothing could stop her now.

Feeling bold, she slid her hands down his chest, wishing she could feel all that expanse of muscle under her fingertips. That there was no barrier between them, that they were skin to skin. She roved her hands over him, greedy to feel every inch. With one hand, she continued farther down, not stopping until she covered his very impressive erection.

Holy wow. Impressive was the only word for it.

He jerked against her hold, tearing his mouth away from hers. He placed his free hand over her hand, stilling her. "I want you to touch me everywhere," he rasped out, as if he was barely hanging on to his control. "But now I need to touch you."

"We can do both."

"I'm on a razor's edge now, beautiful."

She warmed at the endearment, her breath hitching while he started to kneel down in front of her. Oh God, he meant to... Oh, he did.

He stared at the juncture of her spread thighs as if he wanted to devour her. "I love that you're bare." He did that growly thing again.

She had no time to deal with grooming so she got waxed regularly. But that didn't matter. Nothing did except the way he was staring at her as if he might die if he didn't taste her. This had to be the single hottest moment of her life. No one had ever looked at her like that. As if she was the only thing that mattered.

But this man, this virtual stranger who scared and turned her on simultaneously, had all her nerve endings tingling, ready for him to—

He leaned forward, flicking his tongue along her folds, and she lost all ability to think.

He growled against her slick folds, teasing them as she fell back against the counter, spreading wider for him. Her feet dug into his back as he slid two fingers inside her, eating her out as he stroked his tongue against her clit.

"Yes," she managed to get out. "Yes, yes." It was perfect. Almost. The pressure was so close she couldn't stand it.

She shouldn't be close to climaxing. Even the thought of that was crazy. But her body was primed as she teetered on the edge of orgasm.

His tongue. His fingers. His sexy, dirty mouth. It was too much, culminating inside her.

"Your taste," he growled against her in that sexy voice that made her want to strip him naked and taste *him*.

When he started moving his fingers faster and increased the pressure on her clit just a little more, her hips arched off the countertop.

With a firm hand, he reached up, pressed her lower abdomen down, keeping her in place as he continued teasing and torturing her. Soon it was too much. Her orgasm hit hard and fast, her entire body reacting with the pleasure.

So. Much. Pleasure.

Her inner walls tightened around his fingers as she came. Even if she'd wanted to, there was no way to control herself as she writhed against his face and fingers. On her kitchen countertop.

She couldn't believe she was doing this. And she liked it. Scratch that. Loved it.

Eventually, her orgasm started to recede, little pleasure points threading through her entire body as he lifted his head. She was too weak to move, simply laughing lightly as he pulled her up to him.

He kissed her while her come was still on his mouth, making this the second hottest moment of her life. Everything about him was so raw and unfiltered, it was making her brain go haywire. Where had this man been her whole life?

Even as she started to reach for his erection again, he was pulling her skirt down. "What are you doing?" she murmured.

"Told you I wanted you to come."

He'd also said he wanted to taste her pussy. Though it should be impossible, more warmth flooded her as she replayed those sexily growled words in her head.

"I want you to come too."

"I will...later. I wanted that for you."

She blinked. "Why can't I make you come?"

He groaned, laying his forehead against hers. "Because I don't want you to regret anything. And yes, I know you're capable of making your own decisions and know what you want. But...I can't stand the thought of you regretting anything."

She knew she wouldn't. Or she hoped she wouldn't. She'd sort of dived headfirst into this thing with him even though she had no idea where things would lead. Even so, she didn't think she'd regret any of this. "I don't want you to go," she blurted, surprised at herself. She sounded so damn vulnerable and needy and that wasn't her. Not normally. But some of her walls had cracked and she found herself being brutally honest.

"I'm not going anywhere," he murmured, lifting her off the countertop.

"You're staying?"

"All night."

Surprised but pleased, she cuddled up against him as he carried her to the living room. She wasn't sure what he intended for the rest of the night and found she didn't care.

As long as he stayed.

CHAPTER FOURTEEN

—Sometimes the truth sucks.—

L eighton kept Lucy close to him—in his lap—as they sat in her living room. Her condo was plush and in a prime location. With a panel of windows looking down on New Orleans—windows he'd covered with the floor-to-ceiling curtains—a faux fireplace, brightly colored furniture and eclectic accents, the place felt like her. Bright and full of life.

"I think you should reconsider letting me make you come," she murmured, reaching for a small remote control. She pressed a few buttons, and a moment later the fireplace flared to life and soft jazz music streamed in from hidden speakers.

He groaned at her words, burying his face against her neck. Yeah, maybe he should.

When he didn't respond, she continued. "Will you tell me more about yourself? The real you. Not the fake file I have on Spencer Johnson. Or…I'm assuming those details were fake."

He snorted softly. "Yeah, that info is fake." It would stand up under scrutiny, and he was certain that her uncle was having a hell of a time trying to figure out who Spencer Johnson really was. *Good luck hunting, asshole.*

"So…come on."

He felt weird talking about himself. "All right. I grew up…in South Carolina." He wasn't going to give her the name of his hometown just yet. It linked him to Brooks—and if something happened and Lucy was questioned by her uncle, he didn't want that connection out there. "I joined the Marines as soon as I could. Was in for twelve years. Got out a couple years ago."

"Why?" She watched him with her big eyes, her dark hair curled around her face and shoulders in soft waves.

They shouldn't be talking. He should be kissing her senseless, taking her right here in front of the fireplace. Hell, even thinking about it had him getting hard again. But all he had to do was think about the reason he'd gotten out of the Marines and any desire withered. He closed his eyes, sighing.

"You don't have to tell me." Her voice was as gentle as the hand that cupped his cheek.

He covered her hand, held it close for a long moment. "I want to. I want you to know the real me. Not that trust fund jackass cover."

She giggled softly. "Spencer Johnson wasn't a jackass."

Leighton lifted a shoulder. "Well, he wasn't me. I…got out of the Marines not really for one reason. Not…specifically, exactly."

"It's really okay if you don't want to tell me."

But he did. He was just having a problem getting the words out. "After a while, I started feeling drained, I guess. Just, tired all the time. I love the guys I served with and I always thought I'd be a lifer. I think after so many tours I just got burned out. I didn't realize it at the time though."

Once he started talking, it was like he couldn't stop. And she just sat there, patiently listening as she curled up in his lap.

"There was this mission. I can't tell you where or any details, but it was overseas. We were looking for a high-value target. He had information we needed. We'd been staking out this village and...without going into all the details, shit went sideways. People died." He cleared his throat. "Kids died." Closing his eyes, he leaned into her, breathing in her vanilla scent. "It wasn't the first time I'd dealt with that. For some reason, that op just hit me wrong. After the op, I saw some of the pictures from the aftermath. There was this one image of a charred teddy bear missing an eye..."

He took a deep breath and looked at her, trying to force the words out.

"Until that day, I'd always been able to compartmentalize stuff. Or that's what I told myself. So I tried to tell myself that the picture was a teddy bear. But...it wasn't." He couldn't force the rest out. Couldn't voice aloud the lie he'd told himself so he could still function.

But she didn't need him to. "Oh. Oh," she repeated, pulling him into a hug. "I'm so sorry."

He simply leaned against her, breathing in her intoxicating scent. Being held by her grounded him for some reason. "I've never told anyone that."

She hugged him tighter.

He leaned his cheek against hers. "In the end, the outcome we needed from that mission was a failure." And more innocent people had died. He left that part out, not wanting to burden her with anything more. Pulling back, he continued. "It's strange. That day wasn't even the worst op I've ever been on. But something about it just changed me." Jesus, he was like a sieve over here, pouring his guts out, but he couldn't stop himself. "You're a good listener," he murmured.

She gave him a soft smile and thankfully there was no pity in her gaze. Just understanding. She leaned forward and brushed her lips over his once. "Everything you'd been through probably just piled up onto that one day. All that stuff you thought you'd been compartmentalizing? It spilled out. We can only keep our demons at bay for so long."

"You are very smart, Luciana." He liked saying her full name.

She liked it too, if the way her cheeks flushed pink was any indication. "No one ever calls me that."

"It's sexy… You're sexy." That was the understatement of the century. She was this adorable, sweet, sexy woman he wanted to know everything about. He wanted to peel back all her layers.

"So are you."

He just grunted, which made her smile. "Now it's your turn to get personal."

"Well…I'm sure you have a file on me since you and your team, ah…researched my uncle, I guess?"

Feeling guilty, he nodded. "Yeah. But I want what I can't know from a file."

"That's fair." She cleared her throat. "I guess you know about my parents?"

"I do. If it hurts too much—"

"It does hurt, but I have a lot of good memories of them I never get to talk about. Before…before they died, ah, my parents were really great parents. Amazing, actually. I tried half a dozen musical instruments before I realized piano was the only thing I had a real talent for—this was all before I was ten. And they never gave me any grief. I did the same thing with sports, trying to figure out what I liked. Turned out, I'm not so great at the team sports. They let me figure out what I wanted without being pushy. I can admit I was a bit spoiled by them. My dad took me out on a 'date' once a week, just him and his little girl. He also took my mom out once a week, then the two of us out together. And we always had Friday evening game night. He was so giving of his time. They both were."

"It sounds like he loved you both."

"He did. There…was never any hint of anything wrong. Ever. Sometimes my dad would frown when another man would look at my mom too long. Or flirt with her. And she'd just pat his chest and say 'Andrei, you think every man flirts with me' and he'd respond with something like 'I can't blame them, you are the most beautiful woman alive.' My mom would laugh and shake her head but I knew she liked it. My mom didn't work outside the home, but he always told her if she wanted to, she could. Of the two of them, my mom was way more traditional. She'd probably be annoyed with me for how much I work. Though I think my dad would be proud." Sighing, she laid her head against his shoulder. "I haven't talked about them in a very long time. After they died, I just closed off completely where they were concerned."

"Thank you for telling me."

"You're a good listener too, it seems." She sighed as they both watched the crackle of the fake fire in front of them.

"What about growing up with your uncle? Was he…good to you?"

"Knowing what I know now, it feels weird to say it, but yes. He wasn't anywhere close to how my parents had been. Not loving or emotional. But he gave me anything and everything I could have wanted. He sent me to boarding school, made sure I got the best education, got to vacation anywhere I wanted. He took care of my trust and didn't abuse it. He actually helped it grow. But he wasn't my parents. I'm going to sound like 'poor little rich girl' here, but he didn't give me what I needed. What any kid needs. Love and affection. I always strived for his approval." She snorted derisively. "Now that seems ridiculous. What Uncle Alexei thinks doesn't matter," she muttered.

"You are an extraordinary woman."

"Hmm."

He pulled her closer, resting his cheek on top of her head as they both curled up on the couch. After a while, she shifted slightly, settling more against him. She didn't seem to need any more words and he was just fine with the silence. With Lucy, it was comfortable, felt right.

He wasn't sure how much time passed, but soon she dozed, snuggling up against him even closer. She must know she was safe with him. Which she was.

The one thing he knew without a doubt was that he would keep her safe no matter what it took. He just wasn't sure if he should tell her everything he knew.

That her uncle had very likely killed her parents, leaving her an orphan. After what she'd told him about her parents, combined with the information Gage had gotten, it seemed even more likely that her parents had been killed by the man who raised her.

CHAPTER FIFTEEN

—Coffee won't solve all your problems,
but it's a good start.—

Lucy opened her eyes, surprised to find herself in bed—in her rumpled dress. The last thing she remembered was cuddling up to Leighton on the couch after baring her soul to him. He must have carried her in here. And she must have been bone tired to not remember that. More like emotionally drained and ready to sleep for a week.

Sitting up, she stretched, looking around her room. There were no signs of him. He'd probably left. Which…was just as well. She wasn't going to get morose over it.

She wasn't.

Ugh. Swinging her legs over the side of the bed, she started stripping. Her dress definitely needed to be dry cleaned and she needed coffee. Grabbing her favorite silky pink and black robe from the back of her tufted chair by the window overlooking downtown, she headed into the kitchen.

And found Leighton sitting at the island, looking at something on his phone. Oh, and he was totally shirtless.

Which was pretty much all she could focus on as she stared at him. His chest was broad, muscular and nicked with little scars, some faded white with time, others pinker, indicating he'd gotten them more recently. She wasn't sure what he did for a living, not really, but clearly it was very dangerous.

"I thought you'd left," she murmured, stepping into the room.

Natural light filtered down from the high, rectangular-shaped windows that lined the east wall of the room. They were too high for anyone from neighboring buildings to see in, allowing her to enjoy privacy and a lot of light.

He frowned as he pushed back from his chair. "I'm not leaving you."

There was something about the way he said those words that punched straight to her heart. But she shoved those feelings away. People left. It was simply the way life was. Nothing was permanent. "Hmm. Do I smell coffee?"

Half-smiling, he rounded the countertop and brushed his lips over hers, his kiss sweet and possessive at the same time. "I'll make you a cup," he murmured, stepping back. Something about him seemed almost tense this morning.

"Everything okay?" she asked, sitting at the island. She smiled at his neatly folded shirt on the countertop. He must have slept on the couch or in her guestroom.

His back was to her, his shoulders tense as he made a sort of grunting sound. Which definitely wasn't an answer. Maybe he regretted what they'd done last night.

The thought made her cold inside because she'd certainly enjoyed it. And wanted more of it. Not that she should even be thinking of that. When she spotted a little color of...something under Leighton's folded shirt, she reached out and pushed his shirt out of the way. There was another file under it. This one was different than the ones he'd given her. The folder itself was greenish-colored, older and faded.

"Ah..." He set a cup of coffee and a bottle of creamer in front of her and gently moved the file over and out of her reach. "I wasn't sure how much creamer you wanted."

"What's in the file? And where did it even come from?" she asked as she started fixing her coffee the way she liked it. She found herself blushing when his gaze dipped to the gap in the top of her robe. The man had made her orgasm last night, had buried his face between her legs and teased her until she came. She shouldn't be blushing over a heated look.

"Ah. Gage dropped this off." He looked more than just a little uncomfortable as he picked up his own mug and took a long sip of his coffee.

"Well that doesn't answer my other question." When he didn't respond, she sighed. "If you don't want to tell me, it's fine." She wasn't going to push. Lucy had so much on her plate right now, most of which she didn't want to deal with. She wasn't sure she could handle more.

"It's not that. I simply don't know if I should tell you." He scrubbed a hand over his face, tension radiating from him in a way that couldn't be faked.

Her radar started pinging. "Should I be scared? What's going on?"

"Not scared. It's...there's something in this file that will hurt you. Not physically. I just...I don't know if you need the information."

She frowned. "I don't like people making decisions for me."

"And I don't want to make this one for you. After last night, I don't want secrets between us. Not any more than necessary," he added.

"Is it about my uncle? Those girls?"

"Your uncle. And...your parents."

Dread settled inside her, its roots spreading out with angry little stabs. "My parents?"

"Yeah." His jaw was tight, his dark eyes filled with concern.

"My parents are dead." Something he very well knew even before her confession last night. The words came out stilted as chunks of ice broke off in her veins. What could he possibly have to tell her?

"I know what you've thought your whole life. And the official police report backs it up."

She blinked at his words. "Let me see the file."

His jaw clenched again, but he plucked it up and slid it over to her. "I'm sorry," he said simply. "So sorry."

Those roots inside her spread out, twisting her insides up as she opened it. There were the basic notes from the local police department and the name of the detective who'd been in charge of the case. Then there was an official report from an FBI agent named Daniel Jones related to her parents. Her father specifically. And the report had nothing to do with his suicide. Not really. She started scanning the scribbly little notes from the agent talking about a witness. She flipped the page and froze for a moment. Her father's handwriting. *He* had been the witness.

She'd know that bold script anywhere. The paper was clearly a copy of the original but the paper showed the faded age of the copy, a little brown around the edges. Her father had liked to leave little notes for her mom and Lucy, telling them to have a good day. Telling them he loved them. Telling her to make smart choices and to be kind to people. She'd found some other notes after... Well, after. Notes to her mom. They'd been a lot more intimate, though not too much for her to read. They'd been sweet and full of poetry. Not the words of a man who planned to kill his wife and then himself.

And leave his daughter an orphan.

She continued reading and found her hands getting clammy, a chill invading her entire system as she took in her father's words. He'd made a statement to an FBI agent. He'd made the difficult decision to turn on his own brother, Alexei Kuznetsov. Not because he didn't love his brother. But because what his brother had done was wrong. He'd killed a man who wouldn't pay protection money. Mr. Sokolov.

Oh God, she remembered Mr. Sokolov and his family. He'd had two little girls. This had been back when her parents and uncle had been making decent money, but nowhere near the kind her uncle made now. They'd been upper middle class back then and had run a few shops downtown.

Her father went on to say in his statement that the reason he was coming forward was because Mr. Sokolov was a father just trying to provide for his family. It was so eloquent, so very much her dad. *This* was the man she remembered. The man who'd loved and adored her mother. The man who'd taken her out for special ice cream dates and told her she was lucky to be an American but that she couldn't ever forget where her parents had come from, that she had such a rich history. That she could be anything she wanted when she grew up. An astronaut if she chose.

Tears welled up but she brushed them away as she kept reading on to the next page. He'd given the FBI everything he had, but unfortunately they wanted more. An actual confession from her uncle. And her sweet, wonderful papa had agreed to wear a wire in an attempt to get that confession.

She flipped to the next page, then the next. And on and on. There was a whole page of notes from Agent Jones on how he suspected that her uncle had staged the murder/suicide. Some of the coroner's notes didn't feel right so he'd gone to question the coroner.

And the coroner had been found dead from an apparent mugging gone wrong. And the detective who'd been assigned to the case? Also dead. By carbon monoxide poisoning. A "tragic accident." The agent thought the detective had been dirty though. And that her uncle had killed him simply to tie up loose ends. By then her parents' bodies had been released into her uncle's care and cremated. Even if the Feds had wanted to do their own autopsies, it would have been impossible.

Oh God. Oh God. He killed them.

Lurching up, she shoved the papers away, racing for the sink. She threw up the little coffee she had and kept dry heaving as a strong, steady hand rubbed up and down her spine in a soothing motion. Leighton was murmuring something in soft tones, though she couldn't make out the actual words.

"He killed them," she whispered, finally lifting her head from the sink. She felt hollowed out as she stood.

"It's not a hundred percent but..." Leighton's voice was quiet, soothing.

"He did." She fully stood, looked up to meet his gaze. "It makes more sense than my father killing my mother. I...just accepted it because I was thirteen. But it never made sense to me then. There was *never* any violence in my house. Just love. Oh God, my papa never would have killed her," she sobbed out and found herself enveloped in strong, comforting arms.

Lucy wasn't sure how long she cried, but she couldn't stop herself. She cried for her parents, for the life they could have had, for all the years she'd spent hating her father for what he'd done. She cried until the light shifted slightly and she had no more tears.

She had nothing to say, couldn't find any words as she pushed back from Leighton. She didn't want him to leave, but she also couldn't find anything to say right now.

She turned from him, stumbling from the room, not quite sure where she was going. When she found herself in her bathroom, she turned the shower to hot and quickly brushed her teeth to get rid of the taste in her mouth. She got in before it had time to heat up. The cold water blasted her, but she barely felt it. When it turned from cold to hot, she let it beat against her shoulders and back as she stood there, steam billowing around her.

"Lucy?" She heard Leighton's voice from outside the huge tiled shower, but she ignored him.

"Are you okay... I mean, obviously you're not okay." He said something else that she couldn't hear, then, "Jesus, Lucy, I'm so sorry. I shouldn't have told you."

"No. I'm glad you did," she found herself saying. She felt as if she'd lost ten pounds from all the crying, as if she might fall over, but at the same time, she knew in her heart that her father had never killed her mother. That he hadn't hurt her sweet mama. Hadn't left Lucy all alone. She'd known it, deep down she had, even as she'd hated her father.

Or thought she had. She closed her eyes, taking in a breath to steady herself. No way her father would have hurt her mother or her. Her heart, her instinct, knew that.

"I'm coming in." Leighton stepped into the enclave of the big walk-in shower.

The huge shower was one of the reasons she'd bought the condo. It was a certifiable luxury. He averted his eyes and didn't seem to care that his jeans were getting soaked.

"I don't know if you should be alone. Are you...okay? Truly?" So much concern laced his words, his eyes still averted as he basically covered them.

The sight of this strong, wonderful man covering his eyes was somehow absurd. "You don't have to look away. You can...get undressed and join me." The words came out strong because she meant them.

His gaze snapped to hers, those dark eyes sparking fire. "What?"

"You're already halfway there. Just..." She motioned to his pants. He started to protest and she shook her head. "If you say some bullshit about not wanting to take advantage of me, I'm not liable for what I might do."

He still looked as if he wanted to protest, but he moved quickly, stripping off his jeans and well, nothing. Because he had on nothing under his jeans. Damn, that was sexy.

She stared in awe for a long moment as his thick, full cock curved upward against his lower abdomen.

Holy. Hell.

She hadn't been sure what she'd been asking of him until this moment. She thought she'd just wanted someone to hold her in the shower. Now...she needed a whole lot more. But it couldn't be because he felt sorry for her.

Lucy looked into his dark eyes as he moved farther in the shower. Little water droplets bounced off that rock-hard chest she wanted to kiss and lick. "I don't want your pity," she rasped out. "Be here because you want it."

He blinked in true surprise. Then he let out a harsh laugh. "Pity? Not possible," he growled. "I want you more than any woman. Ever. I don't want you to regret me."

"Regret...you?" Had he looked in the mirror lately?

Leighton settled his hands on her hips as he tugged her close. He wasn't sure why she was surprised. The woman was not only stunning, but kind and authentic. And he felt all fucked up and broken. Of course he was worried she'd regret this.

But he wasn't walking away. He wasn't that noble. And Lucy called to a part of him he thought was dead. He'd been on autopilot the last couple years.

He sure as hell wasn't on autopilot now. "I should get out of here. I should...but I don't want to. I won't. Unless you tell me to."

"Kiss me," she softly demanded, her eyes flaring with heat and hunger. For him.

Any control he had, any thoughts of walking away disappeared with those two words. He dipped his head, forcing himself to go slow right now. He didn't want to scare her off, didn't want to screw this up.

Because he wanted more than just today, more than simply now. Even if it was insane to contemplate a future with Luciana, he didn't care. He simply knew that he wanted her in his life, wanted to be part of hers.

Her tongue teased against his, hot and insistent as she pressed her naked body up against his. The woman was absolute perfection, a petite, curvy bombshell who was currently rubbing her breasts against him.

Grabbing her hips, he hoisted her up and pushed her against the wall, growling when she moaned into his mouth. Her nipples were hard little points against his chest as she arched into him.

She wrapped her legs tight around him as he kept her pinned in place. He could kiss her all morning and never tire of it. Hell, he could kiss her all damn day. Her taste was addicting.

She was addicting.

Palming one of her breasts, he savored the fullness as he rolled his thumb over her nipple. She shoved out a breath, her legs tightening a fraction as he did. Oh, she liked that.

What he wouldn't give to simply sink into her right now, but first he wanted her worked up. He was desperate for her and wanted her to be the same for him. His cock was heavy between them, pressing against her abdomen as he dipped his head to her other breast.

Last night he'd gotten to taste her pussy, to make her come. He couldn't believe he'd had any restraint and had actually stopped her from touching him.

"Touch me," he demanded as he sucked her nipple into his mouth.

She raked her fingers down his back, over his chest and arms, as if she couldn't get enough of him. The feel of her hands all over him was making something short-circuit in his brain. Her touch was light, delicate and driving him crazy.

When she reached between them and wrapped her fingers around his erection, he lifted his head to look at her.

Her back arched, as if she missed his kisses, but he kept strumming her other nipple. "I'm clean," he rasped out, realizing they'd never had the conversation. Hell, he hadn't thought sex was on the table. And right about now he wanted to kick his own ass for not having a condom.

"I am too. And I'm on the pill." Her voice was raspy, unsteady.

"We'll wait for sex. I'll run down to the store and grab protection—"

"I want you in me now." Again with that little demand to her tone. "I trust you."

Hell. He believed her about being on the pill, but the fact that she trusted him about being clean? With everything between them, with everything going on in her life…it humbled him beyond belief. Part of him wanted to insist that she let him go grab something, but fuck him. He really *wasn't* noble apparently.

He wanted to claim her, to mark her as his right now. The concept was beyond ridiculous. Sex was sex. Always had been. But this felt different. Because she was different.

She mattered to him.

"This is more than sex to me." He wanted the words out there so there was no mistaking how he felt.

She leaned up and kissed him hard, pressing her body fully to his as she writhed against him. With her mouth and hands on him, it was impossible to think about anything else.

Reaching between her legs, he cupped her mound and found her soaking. For him. He groaned as he slid a finger, then two inside her. Holy hell, she was so damn wet.

She bit his bottom lip, and not gently, making him jerk in surprise. When she grinned wickedly at him, he nearly came right then.

But he wasn't embarrassing himself, no matter how long it had been. Hell no, he was going to experience all of her.

She shifted her body against him and the tile wall even as he moved with her. Then he was inside her, thrusting, over and over as she clung to him.

He kept one hand against the wall as water beat down around them, keeping his balance as he continued thrusting into her. She was so damn tight and slick and all he wanted was to feel her coming around him.

"Oh, God," she rasped out against his neck.

"Say my name." He was desperate to hear it, especially now that she knew his real name. Not some bullshit made-up name.

"Leighton." Her voice was unsteady as she moaned it out. "I'm close."

Yeah, so was he. So damn close he could barely stand it. His balls were pulled up tight as he continued thrusting. He reached between them again and rubbed his thumb over her clit. After last night he had a good idea what kind of pressure she needed.

She jerked wildly against him, her fingers digging into his back even as she nipped at his shoulder. "Right there!"

Even as he drove into her like a man possessed, he continued teasing her. Her inner walls tightened around him harder and harder as she neared her release.

He was close too, barely holding himself back as she clung to him for dear life. When she finally found release, her climax hit hard and fast, her back arching off the wall as she cried out his name.

He watched her come, mesmerized by everything about her. Her long, dark hair hung around her in thick, wet ropes, tangled around her shoulders and breasts.

When she finally opened her bright blue eyes, he swore his heart stopped for a second. Just full-on stopped as she looked at him with the most satisfied, happy expression.

Good. He wanted to wipe away any and all sadness, even for a little bit.

She reached around and gripped his ass hard. "Your turn."

He couldn't help it as a short laugh escaped. God, she was demanding. And probably bossy. And he loved it. She could boss him around all she wanted as long as she was naked and wrapped around him.

He began moving again and all higher brain function stopped. It was just him and her right now in this shower. No outside world, no lies, nothing else.

It didn't take long for him to find release, for the pleasure of her tight sheath around him to push him over the edge. He pressed her against the wall, still keeping a hand against her back so he wouldn't hurt her as he came long and hard inside her.

He felt like he came forever, as if he lost brain cells right then and there.

"That was..." She took a deep breath as she loosened her legs around his waist.

He eased her down onto the tile, careful to hold on to her in case she was as unsteady as he was. "I hope that sentence has a good ending."

She snorted softly and pressed her face against his chest. The water was still warm and pounding down around them, but he was pretty sure she didn't even realize it. "Incredible. Intense. And probably a little insane," she murmured, looking up at him with a hint of apprehension in her gaze.

He cupped her cheek. "It was perfect. And I'm not walking away from this. From us." Let her make of that what she wanted. He wasn't sure what the future held, of what would happen with her uncle, but he wasn't walking away from Lucy.

He didn't think he could.

CHAPTER SIXTEEN

—It's cute that you think I'm asking for permission.—

Lucy paused the recording on her computer—one of the files that Leighton or his team had gotten from someone in the FBI—as her phone rang. She was tired of listening to the monotonous recordings of her uncle talking with various people. It wasn't doing her any good, and hearing his voice only enraged her now. It was probably better that Leighton hadn't told her about what her uncle had done before she'd met with him. She wasn't sure she could have seen him and acted normal. Leighton had left an hour ago to run an errand so she was using the opportunity to acquaint herself more with the files he'd originally given her.

When she saw Nathan's cell phone number, she answered immediately. "Hey."

"Hey, yourself. How's your day off?"

"Pretty good." She kept her tone light and easygoing. What was going on in her life was no one's business, especially not someone she worked with.

"Good. You deserve the time off."

"So what's up?" Because Nathan wouldn't be calling unless there was an issue. They were friendly and she liked him, but they were coworkers, not friends. And she was his boss so she was always aware of that line.

"Your uncle is at the hotel today and he's in a mood," Nathan whispered.

"Oh yeah? How bad?" Nathan was one of the few employees who knew they were related.

"Eh. He's normally brusque, but he seems ragey today. I saw him berating one of the security guys and he made one of the cleaning crew cry. I know you can't do anything about it, but I thought you'd want to know. To maybe...smooth things over later."

Lucy saw her uncle in a totally different light now so it was taking all her restraint not to voice her own anger at him. "Thanks for letting me know. Can you text me the names of the employees he upset?"

"No problem."

"Hey, since I've got you on the phone... You know that file we've got of old security logins? Will you send me a screenshot of a few of the old ID cards?"

"Ah, yeah."

"Thanks." She knew he was curious why but she definitely wasn't going to tell him. "And keep this between us."

"No problem. I'm on break in a few minutes so I'll send the info then."

"Thanks." She had the ability to reactivate old ID logins using one of the security guys' passwords and credentials. Which she'd learned by accident. She felt like a jerk for using someone else's login, but Miller was on vacation right now so it was a perfect time.

She rarely worked from home, but with this info she had the capability to log in to the security panel—on a

COVERT GAMES | 177

limited basis. But she would have enough access to the old security feeds, which was what she wanted. She could of course do it using her own login, but she didn't want this traced back to her. And since Miller was on vacation, he wouldn't get in trouble if anyone found out about this. Not that they should regardless. The only reason anyone should notice this was if they were watching this particular employee. Since she didn't trust that her uncle or security wasn't watching her, this was how it needed to play out.

Once she'd plugged in the right information, she started running various searches including ones using her uncle's face. But also of her uncle and Atkins, as well as others. Maybe she'd come up with nothing, but maybe she'd come up with something the Feds could use. At this point, she was willing to try anything. Because it wasn't as if she had access to her uncle's financials or…anything. This hotel was the only thing she could look into.

At the sound of her front door opening, she paused until she heard, "Lucy, it's me."

Her heart skipped a beat at the sound of Leighton's voice. Which was ridiculous, but there it was. After last night, and this morning, she was seriously hooked on this man.

Whether or not that was wise was a whole other issue. "I'm in my room." A place he was now very acquainted with. After the shower this morning, they'd sort of rested before jumping each other again. Twice. Sex was probably the best distraction from all the other insanity in her head right now. It was taking all her control not to go see her uncle, to confront him right now.

But that would be stupid and accomplish nothing. Well, nothing other than putting herself in danger. No, he was going to pay for what he'd done. She had some dark thoughts about how she would accomplish that, but she was pushing those down. Because killing him, hurting him physically? No. He needed to go to jail for all his crimes. He needed to be locked away in a cage forever. That would be a better punishment for him than a simple death.

Leighton strode in carrying a small white bag. Whatever was in it smelled delicious. "Is that for me?" she asked, moving her laptop to the side. The programs were already running and would dump the files into a folder in the cloud when finished.

He leaned against the doorframe, his half-smile wicked as he seemed to drink her in with that hungry gaze. "Maybe."

She pushed up on her knees. "What's inside?"

He opened it and peered inside as if he didn't know exactly what was in there. The scent was stronger now so it must be really fresh. "A piece of blackberry-orange cake, an assortment of mini muffins—just out of the oven—and some bite-sized apple pie things."

Her stomach rumbled at the thought of all of it. "Not the healthiest dinner, but I'll take it."

"Oh, will you?"

She narrowed her gaze. "You just brought food here to tease me with?"

"Oh, I plan to tease you…" Frowning at his ringtone, he pulled his cell phone out, then let out a short curse. "I've got to take this," he murmured, holding out the bag. "Save some for me."

"No promises." She plucked the bag from him as he took the call, leaving him in her room.

Heading for the kitchen, she decided to make coffee to go with the pastries. He kept his voice low as she walked away so she wasn't sure who he was talking to.

But something told her his conversation had to do with her uncle.

* * *

"What's up?" Leighton had just checked in with the team less than ten minutes ago when he'd been out grabbing food for Lucy and him. He'd been careful to leave out a side exit and, thanks to Gage, had been able to avoid security cameras.

"The tracker is finally on the move," Gage said. "And Colt and Skye are already tailing Leroux."

The smuggler they'd seen talking to Broussard. "Where's it headed?"

"Not sure yet. Looks as if it could be the Garden District. Which isn't too far from where Maria thought they might have been held. We're en route."

"Who's we?"

"Me, Axel and Savage. Brooks is hanging back in case shit goes sideways."

Yeah, Leighton understood that. They didn't need to accidentally show their hand and have Brooks show up on Kuznetsov's radar. And three guys wasn't enough, especially if this was a trap. He didn't think Lucy would set them up, but he wanted to be there. "I'm in."

"I'll send the coordinates to your phone. You can follow the tracker live, the same as us. You got your gear with you?"

"Yeah." He looked up as Lucy entered her room, watching him closely. He tried not to think about her, about what they'd done just hours ago on the bed he was standing next to. "I'll be on my way in two minutes."

She frowned as he hung up. "You're leaving?"

"Yeah." He paused for a moment, wondering how much he should tell her. *Screw it.* "The tracker you planted on Marco is on the move."

Her eyes widened slightly. "That's great."

"Yeah, which means I've got to head out."

"What are you going to do?" she asked, falling in step with him as he headed for her front door. His op bag was waiting in the untraceable SUV he'd parked a few blocks over in a paid parking lot. He had enough gear and weapons for himself—and a team.

"Not sure yet. Follow it and see if the women are being held wherever the tracker stops."

"I'm going with you." Lucy grabbed her black peacoat and started buttoning it up as she reached for a dark pair of sneakers sitting next to five-inch heels by her front door.

"No, you're not. You're not trained, you're not—"

"I don't mean I'm going to infiltrate or whatever with you, but I'm freaking going. I can wait in the car. Try and stop me." Shoes on, she stood, her expression defiant.

Fuck. He shouldn't bring her. He definitely, definitely shouldn't. But he'd seen that program she'd been running on her computer in her room, and was pretty certain she'd made herself a damn target if her uncle was keeping tabs on her. He couldn't leave her alone. "You stay in the vehicle," he said, his tone more forceful than he'd ever used with her. But he didn't care. "Your safety comes first. You don't get out for anything."

Wide eyed, she simply nodded.

"We'll have to do something about covering your hair too. You can't look like you," he muttered more to himself before he leaned down and kissed her. Hard.

She leaned into him automatically, grabbing the collar of his shirt as she held him close. The kiss was over way too soon, but there was no time for anything else.

"You can drive," he said as they hurried down the hallway. She was a hell of a lot more familiar with the city and he'd be able to gear up on the way.

"The elevator is that way," she said, frowning, even as she kept up with him.

"We're taking the stairs. There's an exit we can use where you won't be seen, and I don't want a record of you leaving with me. You can't be seen with me."

Her expression solemn, she nodded. "I didn't even think of that."

Yeah, because this wasn't her world. And he hated that she'd been dragged into it. But there was no going back now. "You're also going to tell me what the hell kind of program you're running on your computer."

Her gaze narrowed again as they raced down the stairs. "Your tone is awful bossy right now."

"Sorry," he muttered. "I'd like it if you would tell me. I don't want you painting a target on your back."

"I don't even care anymore. I want to bring him down. I want him in jail. For the rest of his life."

There was no need to say his name. Leighton knew exactly who she meant and agreed. Though he'd be fine if the man was dead. Hell, maybe dead would be better. Then he wouldn't be a threat to anyone ever again.

CHAPTER SEVENTEEN

—Own your decisions.—

"I can't believe you let her come," Gage said, annoyance tingeing his voice for the first time in a long time. At least toward Leighton.

He'd noticed that all his friends had been almost careful with him the last year or so. Which was ridiculous. "I couldn't leave her by herself," Leighton said into the earpiece. "Besides, she's parked a couple blocks away. "If shit goes sideways, she's fine." And out of the line of any potential fire.

They were all using ear comms to communicate since they were spread out around the house where Marco's tracker had stopped. It was a three-story Victorian home not quite in the Garden District as they'd originally thought, but a little on the outskirts. The area was nice enough and he was certain that the house would sell for a lot but there was a lot of foliage in the front and backyard. The entire neighborhood was set up that way. Most of the homes were older, some in disrepair, some very clearly abandoned, given the boarded-up windows and doors.

Which was good and bad. They could use all the natural cover to their advantage to infiltrate but all that foliage could hide things. Like people and traps. They had no idea what they were walking into at this point. This could be where the women were being held or it could be nothing. Just some place Marco came to for...whatever. Or the house could be rigged and they were all about to get blown up. The last one was doubtful, considering the heat signatures they'd seen in the house using their next-gen FLIR binoculars that Skye had "liberated" from the CIA when she'd left.

Apparently Gage wasn't through complaining because he continued. "Just because your girl was running some programs on her computer—"

"Shut the hell up," Axel said, his tone neutral. "He brought her and that's that. If we all get shot up, she can be our getaway driver so it's not the worst thing in the world to have her here. And I'm tired of your bitching. I seriously don't know how Nova puts up with your ass. Maybe we should nominate her for sainthood."

Leighton smiled to himself. Axel had naturally integrated into their crew with ease. He'd become one of them quickly and gave as good as he got. It was no wonder he and Skye were best friends. Neither of them tolerated bullshit.

"I see movement outside," Savage said quietly. He was on the south side, watching the yard from a tree in the backyard of the house behind it. That house unfortunately wasn't empty but whoever lived there didn't seem to have any dogs or floodlights so he'd been able to scale the tree and use it as his lookout position.

"What do you see?" Leighton asked.

"Just a guy having a cigarette on the back porch. But he's looking around, seems fairly alert. And yep, he's armed. Can't tell exactly what it is, but he's got two bulges on his hips. Pistols likely. Or maybe a pistol and a blade."

"Wonder if he's looking out for anyone," Gage murmured.

Leighton remained in place across the street on the front end. He was directly opposite Savage's location.

The target house had a five-foot-high wrought iron fence surrounding it so even with all the foliage as cover, infiltrating the place would be a pain in the ass. But he'd already figured out a way to use one of the giant oak trees to his advantage. He could simply climb it, then drop down on the other side of the fence. He could be dropping into a trap, but that was the plan.

"Heat signatures haven't changed. I still see six on my end," Axel said. "Two in the midlevel floor and four downstairs. They're clustered around something, the dining room table, it looks like. Or maybe a TV. But there's no other heat signature indicating it's a television so it's like they're eating or waiting."

"Same signatures here too," Savage said. "There's one guy in the back room. Kitchen, I'm guessing. And the guy is still smoking."

"We can take eight guys if necessary," Leighton said.

They all murmured their agreement. "How are we going to do this?" Leighton asked after another ten minutes passed. He was used to being patient, especially after being in the Marines. But they needed to make a decision now. He'd already checked in with Lucy via text and she was fine.

"I say we infiltrate," Savage said. "If there are women inside, I don't like just sitting here."

"We can't make a decision based on emotions," Axel said.

"Fuck that. I'm not going to just sit here," Savage growled.

"I'm just saying, the numbers aren't right. Unless there are six women and two guards. But that seems like too small of an amount, especially given what Maria told us," Axel said.

She'd told them that the guards rotated out, but they almost always had five armed guys at the house at any given time to "keep the women in line." And she said that there had been up to ten women at one point, but some hadn't come back.

"Most of the woman could be working right now," Leighton said.

"Damn it," Gage muttered. "The time is right for that. Which means they could come back with the women and more armed men."

"We could have casualties if we wait," Leighton said, not liking that at all. The whole point was to save the women. To get them all out unscathed.

"Let's do this now," Savage said. "We can take down however many men are in there now. "Then we wait to see if more people return."

"I'm in," Leighton said as the other two murmured their agreement.

"I don't think this should be a front and back entrance. We need to be stealthy about this," Gage said. "Take the power out first, then infiltrate immediately with our NVGs."

Leighton definitely agreed with that. "I can get over the fence from the front and as long as there aren't any motion-sensor lights, I should be able to scale up the house using the bottom balcony railing. I can infil that way, take out the men on the second floor."

"Same here."

"Dude's out back smoking again," Savage said. "I can take him out before we knock out the power. And there's only one guy currently in the kitchen. I can take him out too."

"What kind of force are we using here?" Axel asked.

"If these are the tangos we're after," Leighton said, "lethal. And I can't imagine they're not who we're after, considering Marco's tracker led us here." If these guys worked for Kuznetsov—and according to the run Gage had done once the tracker had stopped here, the home was owned by one of Kuznetsov's many shell corporations—they weren't innocent.

As they finished ironing out the rest of their plan, Leighton moved across the street, using the shadows to cover him. He wasn't a stranger to infiltrating places he didn't belong. Especially behind enemy lines. And that was exactly where they were going, behind enemy lines.

Screw Kuznetsov and anyone who willingly worked for him. He made his money off the pain and suffering of others, had killed his own brother and sister-in-law, leaving Lucy an orphan. God, Leighton wanted to strangle him for that alone.

But he had to be focused now. His life and his teammates depended on it.

Going into hyper-focus mode, he plastered himself against the live oak tree growing next to the fence. Eventually it would grow big enough and push the fence down. He listened to the others talking as he hoisted himself up onto the nearest low-hanging branch, pulling up using all his upper body strength.

This right now was why he kept in shape.

Once he was crouched on the branch, he took a moment to survey his surroundings. The front of the house looked quiet, with two vehicles, including Marco's Audi, parked in the driveway. "Any new movement?" he murmured, keeping his voice pitched low.

"No," Gage said. "Tell me when you're in position and I'll cut the power."

"Affirmative." He stepped out onto the branch, tensing as it creaked slightly. Only two feet to go. Taking another step, he shoved off, propelling himself over the fence and into a cluster of elephant ears. The leaves gave way under his assault but the rustling was minimal.

Still, he paused, looking and listening for any other movement. Even though Gage hadn't scanned any cameras, there was a chance there were some in place regardless. Right now, Leighton was operating as if they were in place. He moved toward the front porch, angling off to the side, and climbed up to the second-floor balcony.

"In place," Axel said quietly.

"Same," Gage said.

"Outside guard down." Savage's voice was barely discernible.

"I'm ready," Leighton said, poised in front of the two French doors on the second floor. They'd all be going in fast and hard now.

"Three, two, power's off."

Weapon up, Leighton shoved his NVGs into place and kicked at the doorjamb. Wood splintered as the flimsy doors gave way. Sweeping the room, he saw no one. Hurried through it.

Pft. Pft. The soft sound of a silenced weapon filled the air. "Tango down on second floor. One ran out of the room, but he's armed." Axel's voice was tight, controlled.

Leighton swept into the hallway, all his muscles tight as he swept into the next room, ready to clear it. He could hear movement downstairs and shouts of alarm, but he tuned it out for now. When the heated outline of a man popped out from behind a big dresser, he swiveled fully, barely dodging to the side as the man fired.

Pop. Pop. Pop. Pop.

Plaster exploded behind him as he dove to the side, landing on the nearby mattress. He fired once, twice, hitting the guy in center mass.

The man dropped, but Leighton kicked the weapon away and shot him once more in the head before stepping out of the room. He tensed when he saw another man, but it was Axel.

Axel raised a fist, but he knew it was him because of the full tactical gear.

"Another down." There had only been two men up-stairs so it should be clear.

"Four down here," Gage murmured.

One left to go. "Let's try and keep this one alive." They needed to question someone about the women.

Leighton moved on silent feet to the stairs, heading downward. When he reached the next landing, a man rounded on him from the first landing, pistol raised.

Shit. He fired, hitting the man in center mass. The guy fell like a stone, not even getting a shot off. So much for keeping him alive. "Last one down."

"Finish sweeping," Gage said. "I'm doing a search for electronics."

On the chance a neighbor heard the shots from the tangos, they might need to run sooner than later.

They swept the house methodically, using their NVGs to guide them. The place was bare, with only two beds, and was nothing like Maria had described. The re-frigerator was empty as well, which didn't sit well with him. This wasn't a place where trafficked women would be kept. They might exploit the women, but she said they'd kept them well fed and had allowed them to exer-cise.

This house looked like...a trap. And none of the men he'd checked had anything to identify them other than a couple TracFones—aka burners. And Marco wasn't here.

"I'm going to grab the tracker off the car," Leighton said as they all convened in the kitchen.

"We'll take fingerprints, see if we can get any hits on them."

Leighton nodded, though he had no doubt these men were affiliated with Kuznetsov. He recognized a few of the tattoos. Some were from local New Orleans gangs, but others were clearly Russia based. So maybe Kuznetsov had some of his guys working with locals. Who knew at this point. He took his NVGs off as he headed outside, careful to scan for anyone watching.

He found the tracker exactly where Lucy said she'd put it. As he snagged it, an SUV screeched to a halt in front of the house.

Leighton turned as a side door opened. Through the bushes and fence, a masked man jumped out with an AR-15 in hand.

Heart pounding, he raced down the driveway along the side of the house. "Shooter outside!" he shouted through the ear comm, bracing for a hit.

Right now they needed to get the hell out of here and not have a showdown with however many shooters there might be. Because there could be more backup on the way than just one guy.

Pop. Pop. Pop. Pop. Pop. Pop.

Bullets pinged off the fence as he rounded the back of the house. Out of the line of fire, but not out of the woods.

"Retreating," Savage shouted.

Leighton joined the others in the backyard as they all ran as one cohesive unit toward the back fence line. "That's more than one shooter," he snapped out. He would know. Hell, they would all know.

192 | KATIE REUS

Shouts erupted behind them in a foreign language. Leighton half turned as they reached the fence line to see three men with automatic weapons.

He stopped, braced himself as he raised his weapon and fired. The one on the far left dropped as a bullet slammed into his chest. He stumbled back under the force, but his vest took the hit. Almost simultaneously, the other two men dropped but not before one of them got another round off.

Bullets sliced through the air, pinging off the house and fence in a macabre rhythm.

"Fuck," Axel gritted out as he gripped his upper arm. Blood spilled over his gloves and down his sleeve.

"We can't leave a blood trail," Gage said. "There can't be evidence we were here." They'd been careful about wearing masks and gloves.

Leighton heard more shouts from the front yard. Backup had arrived.

Leighton and Savage moved quickly, hoisting Axel up and over. Then the three of them jumped over, moving with ease that came from years of training.

Even through the foliage, they could see four more men racing through the backyard. Holy shit, this was some serious backup. They must have tripped some kind of alarm in the house.

"Run!" Gage pulled out a grenade.

It was a crude way to do it, but the explosion would cover up any blood spatter Axel might have left behind on the fence.

They were all moving even before Gage tossed the grenade. Then he tossed another.

As they sprinted across the neighbor's grassy yard, an old man stepped out onto the back porch. He took one look at them and raced back inside, slamming the door behind him.

They were silent as they moved toward the front of the yard. They had to abandon their vehicle, assuming it was compromised at this point. It was clean of prints and couldn't be linked back to them anyway.

Leighton whipped out his burner phone and called Lucy. "Where are you?"

"Same spot. But I thought I heard gunfire. Are you—"

"Meet us on the corner of Eighth and Magnolia," he snapped out. They raced down the sidewalk, dressed head to toe in tactical gear and looking very much out of place. It was the right time that most people would be inside but they spotted a woman walking a teacup-type dog. She screamed when she saw them, scooping her dog up and running across someone's yard. The dog barked frantically.

They continued down the sidewalk in single file order. They'd put those guys off long enough with the grenades that they had a decent enough head start, but they needed to get the hell out of here.

As they reached the edge of the end of the street, the other SUV skidded to a halt.

They all dove in, with Leighton taking the front.

"Oh my God, you're bleeding!" Lucy's eyes were wide as she looked in the rearview mirror at Axel.

"Turn left here," Leighton said.

"The hospital's the other way," she said even as she made the turn, looking in the rearview mirror at Axel again. He was clutching onto his bleeding arm as Savage tried to inspect it.

"We're not going to the hospital," Leighton said, turning back around.

"That's a lot of blood," she said hesitantly. "Maybe we should."

"Toss the tracker," Gage said. "If they discovered it, they might've added something of their own to it just in case."

Damn it, Leighton should've thought of that. He rolled down the window and threw it into oncoming traffic. It would be destroyed soon enough.

"What the heck is going on!" Lucy's voice trembled as she looked over at him.

"It was a setup. Marco or someone must've discovered the tracker and wanted to find out who'd planted it."

"Unless *you* set us up," Savage said quietly from the back.

Before Lucy could respond, Leighton swiveled around. "We've been friends for life. But watch your words now. She didn't set us up." He knew that in his gut.

"I didn't do anything," Lucy snapped out, trembling.

Leighton reached across the center console and squeezed her arm lightly. "Take a right here."

Savage just grunted in the back.

"It's highly doubtful she did any of this," Gage said, looking at the screen of one of the burner phones. "First, one of the men called for backup during our attack. Second, considering Lucy is currently running security scans on her uncle's image at the casino, that limits the likelihood she's trying to get us killed. Not to mention I've been monitoring all her incoming and outgoing communications."

"What?" she demanded as Leighton pointed for her to take another turn. "So many questions right now. You've been monitoring me?"

"Yes," Gage said simply.

She let out an annoyed, rage-filled growl. "How do you know about the scans?"

"Leighton told me what he saw on your laptop. Speaking of, we need to get to her condo now. We need to grab the laptop."

"Why?" she asked, looking at Leighton for confirmation. He nodded, so she took the next turn. "I know a shortcut there," she murmured to him.

"Because if he even suspects you're the one who planted the tracker, you're not going back there," Leighton said, not needing Gage to answer for him.

"My uncle wouldn't…" She trailed off, swallowing hard. "He *would* hurt me," she whispered. "Oh God, he would kill me." It was as if it was just dawning on her. Likely she'd already understood that, but knowing something and truly understanding it were two different things.

The man had killed her parents. He wouldn't balk at killing her.

Her fingers tightened on the wheel as she continued driving, looking a bit as if she was on autopilot.

"Well, I'm gonna live if anyone cares," Axel muttered from the back seat, more to himself than anyone else, Leighton guessed.

Once they made it to the covered parking lot, he handed her a ball cap and big sunglasses even though it was night out and this was her building.

"Gage, can you—"

"Already on it," Gage said, working on his phone. He'd be able to corrupt the security cameras here easily. "You've got about ten minutes to grab what you need. We shouldn't be here longer than that."

In case someone was in the garage and happened to notice Lucy, he wanted her unrecognizable. Because if her uncle didn't know she was involved with planting the tracker, he didn't want Kuznetsov to find out inadvertently.

Though after tonight, that all might be a moot point. The man could know and could already be after her.

CHAPTER EIGHTEEN

—Not everybody has to like me. I can't force you to have good taste.—

"He's careful," Skye said, looking through her long-range binoculars from their rooftop perch a couple blocks away from the warehouse they'd tracked Leroux to.

"He's a smuggler," Colt replied. And smugglers on the whole were very careful.

"True enough. So...I have an idea," she said.

"For some reason I don't think I'm going to like it." Didn't mean he wouldn't take part in it though. He scanned the surrounding area with his own binoculars. They'd tracked Leroux here and he'd taken a long, circuitous route. He'd made a lot of pointless stops, clearly in an effort to ferret out any tails.

Too bad for him they were pros and he was a midlevel smuggler. The guy was decent enough, according to his reputation, but he wasn't big league. Still, that didn't mean he wouldn't have information they needed.

"I was thinking we can do to him that thing we did in Argentina a few years ago."

It took him a moment then he smiled. "That seems...a bit brutal. The guy's just a smuggler."

"Well, the plan won't be the same. I just mean the same concept. We'll call the cops on him, not thugs who will kidnap and torture him. But this way, he'll be out of our hair and we can break into his warehouse."

He nodded once. "It's a good plan."

She snorted that way she often did. "Of course it is."

"Who makes the call?" he asked.

"I will. I can pretend to be hysterical."

He snorted. He wasn't sure exactly what his wife was going to say, but she was going to get the smuggler arrested. Or if not arrested, at least he'd be detained for a while. So they would be free to break into his warehouse. Because Colt guaranteed the guy had an alarm system. But Leroux wouldn't have an alarm system rigged to the security company. No, he'd have it rigged to his own phone. But he wouldn't be able to do a damn thing about it going off when he was in police custody.

"He's leaving now," Skye said, still looking through her binoculars. "I'm making the call." She pulled out one of the burners and started to breathe erratically.

He could hear the operator on the other line as Skye said, "Oh my God! Oh my God! I just saw a woman kidnapped! This man punched her in the face and threw her in the back of his SUV. It looks like he tied her up." Still talking in that hyperactive tone, Skye went on to give a crystal-clear description of the man right down to what type of shoes he was wearing. "I know what shoes they are because my brother has the same pair." There was a pause and then Skye said, "I saw his license plate too!

Will that help?" she asked, and he could see her trying not to laugh.

Because of course it would help.

She rattled off the license plate that they'd memorized earlier and then when the woman asked for her name and location, Skye said, "Oh my God! He's turning around." She quickly rattled off the street name. "Oh God, he sees me!" Then she hung up and smashed the burner under her foot.

"Well, if that doesn't work, we'll come up with a new plan," Colt murmured.

"It'll work. They'll definitely send a few uniforms his way regardless. I figure we've got about ten minutes until he's pulled over."

"Just enough time to grab the van." They'd "borrowed" a van from a parking lot and switched the plates for this job.

Ten minutes later, they stood in front of the side door of the nondescript warehouse.

"There are a couple wireless cameras," Skye murmured.

"Yeah, saw that," he said quietly, keeping his head down and angled away from the ones he'd seen before they approached.

"I recognize the type. It will definitely transfer video to his phone."

"That's all right. He won't be able to identify us. No one will." They'd worn disguises for this operation for this very reason. This was the kind of op where they couldn't wear masks. They'd been out in public so they had to blend in.

Skye had a platinum blonde wig on and was wearing four layers of padding underneath a loose-flowing top that made her look about forty pounds heavier than she actually was. She also had on leggings and sneakers, which would make it easy to run if necessary.

He'd worn a ball cap and added cotton to his cheekbones to change the shape. And he had on a wig underneath his hat, covering his ears. The glasses he was wearing would distort his face as well.

Always be prepared. The CIA had drilled that into them long ago.

"He could have the door rigged with a booby trap." Skye paused, glancing down the quiet, nearly empty street. Leroux had chosen this location well. Not a lot of foot traffic and right on the water.

Colt nodded. The chances of that were actually fairly high, considering the guy was a smuggler. He'd be very particular about his stuff and wouldn't mind killing someone to protect it. Because Leroux had clients who valued their privacy.

"I say we blow through a wall instead of going through the door."

Colt grinned, nodding. "You just want an excuse to blow shit up," he murmured, falling in step with her.

They walked around the warehouse, heading for the west side, which didn't back up against anything. It was right on the water, which was a smart place to be. Leroux would be able to move stuff in and out by truck or boat. And it gave him an escape plan if necessary.

"There might be people inside," Skye said.

Maybe. Smugglers tended to operate a certain way and they didn't trust anyone. Not even their own people. All that art and other expensive things just lying around for the taking? It could be too much temptation if one of their subordinates got greedy. "We'll find out soon enough."

Shrugging, Skye started pulling out what they would need to blow a huge, jagged hole into the wall. Once she'd set it all up, they rigged the det cord and ran to the back of the warehouse. Once they were clear, she grinned and set it off.

Then his amazing wife rubbed her hands together gleefully. "It's time to go shopping."

* * *

"How are we doing on time?" Skye asked as she rushed up to the back of the van. They'd reversed it through the hole they'd blown up.

He'd grabbed the majority of the stuff, but she'd gotten antsy being the lookout so they'd traded places. She slid a Monet painting into the back of the packed van.

"This is probably worth a couple mil," she said. "If it's real."

They'd been stealing the most expensive stuff they could find for the last twelve minutes. "Twelve minutes. We need to wrap up in three."

"Done. I want to grab an Egyptian piece I saw a few rows back."

He nodded, peering out the hole and glancing down the side of the warehouse. Still no company, but they shouldn't be here any longer than necessary. It was possible Leroux had contacted someone and sent backup if he was being detained by the police. But fifteen minutes was as far as Colt was willing to go.

When he heard the sound of a distant engine, he pulled out his SIG and peered out the hole. No one. But he heard the engine, then the sound of a door slamming. As he did, Skye moved in behind him.

"What's up?" she murmured.

"I think we have company."

"I'll head to the front door." Her voice was as quiet as his. Then she was off, ghost silent, despite the extra bulk she was carrying. He flipped on his ear comm.

He remained where he was, keeping an eye on the opening. They'd checked and there were only a couple entrances in this place. And the front door had been rigged as they'd suspected. So if someone entered through it, they needed the code.

When his phone buzzed, he glanced at it. It was a text from Gage. *It was a setup. A is wounded. He's okay. We're headed back to base.*

"Get up here now," Skye said quietly into the ear comm.

Hell, he'd have to text Gage later. Weapon up, he used the many aisles filled with stolen goods to cover himself.

He stopped when he found Skye, weapon drawn on a petite, curly-haired woman.

"You're fucking dead for breaking in here," the woman snarled.

It was hard to take her too seriously when she was facedown, hands behind her head.

"Yeah, yeah." Skye rolled her eyes at him when he approached. "Heard it all before. Now listen to me and listen good."

Colt moved into action, restraining the woman's hands behind her back and taking her ID and phone as Skye spoke.

"We've taken a lot from the man I'm assuming is your boss. Some items I can guarantee he'll want back sooner than later. You tell him to call this number." Skye tossed a plain white card on the floor next to the woman's face. A number was scrawled onto it. "If he calls, he gets his shit back. If he doesn't call, I'll set it all on fire and send him a video of it burning. Including that Monet painting."

"You stupid bitch!"

"Thank you," Skye said calmly. "Think you can manage to remember this little message?" She nudged the woman once in the ribs.

"Yes," she said through gritted teeth.

It didn't take them long to clear out. In case the woman had backup on the way, they grabbed just one more piece each and headed to the van.

"You wouldn't really burn that Monet, would you?" Colt asked as he steered out onto the street. They'd already slashed all of the woman's tires, but she wouldn't be going anywhere anytime soon regardless.

Skye looked at him in horror. "Hell no. I'll hang it up next to the crab painting if we don't give it back to Leroux."

He wasn't sure if she was joking.

As he drove, she pulled out a plastic bag from under her oversized top. "These are all the trackers on the various pieces of art and artifacts." She held it up, the small black trackers clicking against each other as she did. "And I have sort of a mean idea."

Oh, he knew exactly what she wanted to do. "You want to send them off in a bunch of directions, don't you?" To send Leroux on a wild goose chase.

"Yes. He won't call us right away. He'll try to figure out who we are and he'll think he's smarter than us and follow the trackers. I give him until about tomorrow morning to make contact. Maybe sooner. It depends on how fast he can mobilize once the cops let him go." Then she gave that evil villain laugh that he loved so much.

Life with her was definitely never boring.

CHAPTER NINETEEN

—Tonight's forecast? Ninety-nine percent
chance of wine.—

L ucy sat at the island countertop of a huge house in
the Garden District. There were a whole lot of people in the house right now, but most of them were in
different rooms. Someone was taking care of the man
who'd been shot. Or, "nicked" as the man had said. She
was pretty sure his name was Axel.

Not that it really mattered. Her life might have more
or less imploded if her uncle had figured out she'd been
involved with tonight. She really wished Leighton was
with her, but he'd asked her to sit tight while he took
care of some things. Like "things" wasn't cryptic. *Ugh.*

"You look like you need a drink," an older man said as
he stepped into the kitchen, carrying a mug. He had
green eyes and dark hair with auburn and gray peppered
through it and appeared to be fit. Like he'd been in the
military at one point. Or maybe still was. Who knew?
"And I'm not talking about coffee," he continued.

"It's late to be drinking coffee anyway."

He shrugged his shoulder. "Never too late for coffee.
So is there anything I can do for you? Leighton is still
tied up."

"You don't have to do anything for me." If the man was here, Leighton must trust him, but she wasn't sure of anything at this moment.

"I know I don't. But you just walked into chaos and I'm guessing you're not used to it."

She gave him a wry smile. "Well, I work at a hotel and casino so that's not completely accurate."

"How do you feel about wine? Or beer?"

"Red wine would be nice." Hell, at this point, she needed something to ease her nerves. Leighton and his friends had gotten into something serious tonight—most of which he hadn't really told her about, but the guy who'd been shot was a big giveaway that it wasn't good—and she felt adrift right now.

He nodded and started rummaging around in a cabinet. She recognized the bottle he pulled out and it was a nice one.

"Leighton tells me you had quite an eventful night."

"Not as eventful as him, I'm sure." Her voice was dry.

The man laughed at that. "True."

"What's your name anyway?"

"I'm sorry, I forgot my manners. My name's Colt. But everyone calls me Senior. My son isn't here, but he should be back soon enough."

Almost on cue, the back door opened up and a man and woman strode in. The man looked like the older one with dark hair and green eyes—though he was holding a ball cap and wig in his hand.

"Hey Dad, I didn't expect you here so soon."

The woman shut the door behind them, a grin on her face as she nodded at Senior. Then, to Lucy's surprise, she stripped off her top, only to reveal a bunch of layers of padding, which she also ripped off to reveal a skintight black tank top underneath. Lucy recognized her as the woman from the hotel. She then ripped off a platinum bob and gave the older man a big hug. "It's good to see you. Sorry I'm all sweaty."

"You two okay?" he asked.

"Yeah. Took care of what we needed to take care of." The woman shot her a quick glance, nodded once.

Lucy was silent, intently listening to their conversation and hoping she might learn something. Her mind might be a jumbled mess but she understood the value of being quiet because people tended to forget about you when you blended into the scenery. She'd learned that at work.

A man she'd met earlier—named Brooks, she thought—came into the room and hugged the woman from behind. The auburn-haired woman looked as if she was in the third level of hell as she stood there accepting the brief squeeze of affection.

"Thanks for bringing my girl in," he said. "She said you set it all up behind our backs."

The woman just grunted and shrugged off his hug.

Brooks simply laughed and clapped Colt on the shoulder once before heading out.

It was like that for the next ten minutes, with people milling in and out, talking about random things she knew nothing about, grabbing food or drinks. It was fairly late, and even though a man had been shot earlier and they'd very clearly gotten into some sort of gun battle, all these people were just going about their business.

Lucy was starting to get edgy, wondering where the hell Leighton was. She wasn't sure where to go or how to extract herself because technically she couldn't leave the place. They weren't even sure if her uncle knew she'd been involved with placing the tracker. They weren't sure of *anything*. Apparently someone was sitting on her condo, keeping an eye on it, and no one had approached her place. At least that was good.

But she hated all this sitting around.

Finally, Leighton stepped into the kitchen, looking exhausted, but he smiled as he met her gaze. "Have you eaten?" he asked, ignoring the two others, Nova and Senior, in the room.

She shook her head. "Wine's fine."

He frowned and headed for the fridge. "You two, clear out," he ordered to the others. "And tell everyone else to stay out of the kitchen for a while. We need privacy."

Nova raised her eyebrows while Senior simply got up. But they both left.

And even though they'd been perfectly polite, a weight lifted from Lucy's chest. "You take care of everything you needed to?"

"Mostly. Had to make some calls," he said as he started pulling out food from the oversized refrigerator. "We've got Chinese or Italian. It's all takeout but fresh."

"Italian sounds good." She hadn't thought she could eat, but right about now she realized she was famished.

"So…can you fill me in more?" she asked as he started preparing two plates of pasta and sausage in a cream sauce and a whole lot of fresh vegetables that looked amazing.

He turned back to her after putting one plate in the microwave. "I reached out to a Fed contact of mine. A friend. I trust her," he added.

Lucy didn't like the weird twinge in her chest when he said "her." Jeez, he could have female friends. She really did need sleep. Or something.

"They have no idea if your uncle knows you planted that tracker. They also say there's nothing linking him to any of the dead men from tonight."

"The Feds know you guys were involved?"

He gave her a dry look. "Hell no. I mean, my friend knows, but not officially, and I haven't admitted anything on the record. It seems your uncle is busy moving certain accounts right now. They've got someone on the inside willing to testify against him but it might not be enough so they're having this person try to get something on the record."

"Like a recording?"

"Yeah."

"Oh, okay."

"They're hoping to get what they need by tomorrow night. There's some deal going down. They don't have the details, but apparently it's big. And they're gearing up to bring your uncle down."

"Good." She hoped he rotted in prison forever.

210 | KATIE REUS

"I can almost guarantee the Feds will want to talk to you."

"Me? Why?"

"You're related to him and work for him." He pulled the steaming plate out and put it in front of her. "Go ahead and start," he murmured before putting his own plate in.

"Thank you. And...that makes sense. I guess I just didn't think about that."

"We've already contacted an attorney to be your representation if and when you talk to them."

"I don't need one." She blew on the bit of pasta on her fork. She hadn't done anything wrong so why would she need a lawyer?

"Yes, you do. And you're not going to talk to anyone in law enforcement without her present."

"Her?"

When he said the woman's name, Lucy blinked. "She's good. Really good. Even I've heard of her."

"Yes, she is. Promise me, no matter what, you won't talk to anyone by yourself." He pulled a piece of paper out of his pocket with the high-profile attorney's name and number written on it.

"I promise." She was definitely in over her head right now. "So...weird question. Of many. I'm supposed to work tomorrow. I should call in, right?" Lucy knew she wasn't a prisoner. Not exactly, but she wasn't sure of what she should be doing right now.

"*Yes.* Until we know more about what's going on."

"What *is* going on? What happened earlier tonight?"

"The place had a bunch of armed men sort of ready for us."

"Sort of?"

"These guys were local thugs, not trained. And the backup were more gang members. But they were waiting for someone. And the Audi was in the driveway with the tracker on it."

"Your Fed friend tell you that? About them being locals, I mean."

"No. We took their fingerprints and ran them. Well, Gage did."

She blinked at that and took another bite. "Does anyone know where Marco is?" He was another one she was certain needed to be in jail.

"Nope. My Fed friend said he's gone to ground."

"Great," she muttered. "What about all those security runs I downloaded? Is there anything useful on them?"

"A couple of the guys are scanning them now. If there's anything linking your uncle to anyone bad, we're forwarding it to the Feds."

Setting her fork down, she rubbed her temple as he sat next to her.

"I'm sorry you're anywhere close to this," he said, reaching out and cupping her cheek. He rubbed his thumb over her skin softly, watching her with an intense expression that made her stomach muscles tighten.

"I'd rather be aware than in the dark."

He nodded as he let his hand drop.

Immediately she missed the feel of his touch. "So I'm staying here tonight, right?"

"Of course. I'm not letting you out of my sight. This is the safest place possible for you."

"Am I staying in your room or do I have one of my own?" she asked carefully. He was being affectionate but she wasn't sure of anything.

He stilled at that. "Whatever you want. You're under our protection no matter what."

"I'd like to stay in your room. I'd really like that."

He shoved out a breath. "Good. I plan on making you come at least twice tonight."

Warmth flooded her cheeks as she speared another bite of sausage. She couldn't believe he'd just said that.

"I love it when you blush," he continued, leaning close and brushing his mouth over hers. "Maybe soon I'll get you to talk dirty."

"Maybe," she murmured, smiling against his soft, perfect mouth.

* * *

"So how many people are even staying here?" Lucy asked as she and Leighton stretched out in front of the fireplace on a tufted, very comfortable blue and cream loveseat. They were on the third floor of the big home and their room was huge. King-size bed, huge bathroom that seemed to hold a lot of the original charm, a small balcony and a little kitchenette that had likely been added on recently.

"Ah...I'd have to count it up. We recently got a few additions."

"Yeah, I gathered that from some of the conversations. The one named Skye surprised some of the men by flying their wives here, right?"

"Yes. She said they were acting like sad pandas and needed to be at full capacity for this job."

Lucy laughed lightly. "So everyone's married?"

"Mostly. Engaged at least. Except Colt's dad. And me, of course. The only one whose significant other isn't here is Savage."

"The one who thinks I set you guys up."

"He doesn't think that anymore." Leighton wrapped his arm around her and pulled her closer.

"So…what's going on as far as the trafficked women are concerned?"

Leighton made a frustrated sound. "We'd hoped to find them tonight."

"Instead you walked into a trap."

"Not a great trap, thankfully," he murmured, kissing the top of her head.

She turned slightly to look up at him. "How are you doing? I know men shot at you. I'm really trying not to ask too many questions but…are you okay?"

He rolled his head back, looking up at the ceiling, pausing for a long moment. "We infiltrated the home. All the men were armed. They fired on us, we fired on them…they're all dead, and I killed two of them."

Oh. Wow.

He looked at her, his expression shuttered. "It's not the first time and it won't be the last."

"I'm glad you're okay," she whispered.

Leighton blinked. "You're not...disgusted?"

"No." Maybe she should be but...what she knew of this man, he didn't seem like he'd kill unless it was in self-defense or to protect someone. "What happens with the women now? You said the Feds might be bringing my uncle down tomorrow. But I also remember what you said about him basically cutting his losses and getting rid of 'evidence.'"

He sighed, looking back at the fire. The shadow from the flames danced off his handsome face. "We're still working on that. Colt and Skye might have a lead on where they are. Or, they're hoping to soon."

"Does that have anything to do with them coming in wearing disguises?"

He snorted softly. "Yeah. If they do get a lead on where the women are being held, I'll have to leave. And I can't take you with me."

"I get it. Completely." And she did. Sighing, she laid her head on his shoulder. "I feel so useless right now."

"Yeah, me too."

"You just kicked ass a couple hours ago."

He let out a short laugh. "I don't like having to wait."

She didn't either. "Maybe we could get to know each other better. I don't actually know your last name. I understand if you can't tell me—"

"Cannon. It's Cannon. And I probably shouldn't tell you." He kissed the top of her head again. "I just don't give a fuck."

Warmth spread through her at his brusque tone. "Thank you for trusting me. Now that I know that, I have a more important question. What's your favorite flavor of ice cream?" It was a silly thing, but she wanted to know a lot more about him.

"Strawberry," he answered without pause.

"Interesting."

"Good interesting?"

"Yes. Mine's Mississippi Mud."

"I've never had it," he murmured.

"We'll have to remedy that," she murmured, lifting her head slightly to look at him. Being with him felt right on a level she wasn't sure she grasped yet. While she felt adrift in general after everything she'd learned, being with Leighton grounded her, made her feel sane.

His gaze fell to her lips and he looked as if he wanted to kiss her, but he cleared his throat instead. "Tell me something about yourself I won't know from the file."

Disappointment lanced through her, but she settled back against him, enjoying the warmth of the small fire. "I play piano pretty well. I know I told you I took lessons, but I never stopped playing. There's a great baby grand at the casino I practice on a few days a week. What about you? Tell me something about you."

"I have no musical talent, but I like camping. Just disappearing into the wilderness for a week or so with a tent, supplies and myself."

"That sounds…horrible."

The warmth of his laughter wrapped around her, infusing her. "So that'll be something we won't do together."

She loved that he was talking about them in the future tense. "Maybe glamping."

"Yeah, maybe."

After a few minutes of silence, he said, "I know you didn't ask, but my parents aren't part of my life. My dad does offshore drilling off the Gulf Coast. When I was young, he used to come home when he had leave, but my mom cheated on him—something I didn't realize until I was older—and he stopped coming home altogether when I was about twelve. My mom stuck around until I was eighteen, barely. Then she split."

"Where'd she go?"

"No idea. Last I heard she was living in some sort of spiritual commune or whatever the hell in India. But that was two years ago."

"Do you want to find her?"

"No. I learned early that sometimes it's better to have no family than shitty family."

"The people in this house seem like your family."

"They are. Not by blood, but they're definitely my family."

Lucy didn't respond for a while as she digested his words. "You trusted me with your real name even before my uncle has been arrested." And she really hoped he would be soon.

"Yeah."

She sat up, shifting until she straddled him. She wasn't going to wait for him to make a move this time. "If I was working with my uncle, I could give him that information, let him know your real name, and that would put your friends—your family—in danger."

"I trust you." It was as if it was that simple. And maybe it was.

She felt insanely humbled that he trusted her. Her entire world had been ripped apart in the last few days and she was patching and stitching it back together, and Leighton was threatening to pull her apart again. But in a much different way. She'd seen the world a certain way for so long, had been so certain of things. Now she was reevaluating everything.

Before she could get too lost in her head, Leighton kissed her, his tongue plundering and teasing as she started grinding against him.

With him, it seemed it didn't take long to get her worked up. Not long at all.

CHAPTER TWENTY

—Why fight a good thing?—

Leighton half-smiled at Brooks, who was working on his laptop at the island countertop. "Hey, surprised you're down here." Meaning, now that Darcy was here.

Brooks raised an eyebrow. "I could say the same thing about you."

It was no secret that Leighton and Lucy were sleeping together so, fair enough. "Yeah, couldn't sleep. Hazel says they're supposed to bring Kuznetsov down by tomorrow night but he's a slick bastard." And Leighton was on edge.

Brooks nodded once. "That's why I'm awake too. I know I've got a truce with Kuznetsov but if he finds out I'm here and we went after his people, I know what will happen."

"We'll just kill him if he does," Leighton said, because there would be no other option at that point.

Brooks simply grunted a non-response.

If Kuznetsov found out they were involved, there would literally be no other choice but to end him. Leighton thought the guy deserved to die anyway, but he also deserved to pay for his crimes. His victims deserved to have justice. But not at the risk of putting any of their friends or family in danger. Because a man like Kuz- netsov was vengeful and would come after Brooks's fam- ily to hurt him.

"How's your dad?" he asked, wanting to change the subject.

Brooks gave a wry smile. "He's fine. He's got Martina with him at his place—she's living there now anyway since they're engaged. Plus, he convinced Olivia, Valen- cia, Mercer, Mary Grace and obviously the baby to all stay over. Just in case things go sideways, everyone is se- cure."

"Good. Can I ask you something?" he asked.

His lifelong friend nodded. "Of course."

"You fell for Darcy fast. I mean, you screwed things up, but eventually you won her back."

"Is there a question in there anywhere?"

"Sorry, man. I just…"

"You've fallen for Lucy?"

"Yeah. I don't understand how I feel *so much* for her. We haven't known each other long. But she's under my skin. I can't…imagine walking away from her after this operation. I want her in my life. I want to be in *her* life."

Brooks lifted a shoulder in that stoic way of his. "When you know, you know. If she's it for you, don't fight it."

He simply nodded and paused as Darcy stepped into the kitchen, half awake. "What are you doing?" she asked her husband sleepily. "It's two in the morning."

"Your snoring woke me up," Brooks deadpanned.

Leighton half laughed and slid off the chair. It was definitely his cue to leave.

"I do *not* snore," Darcy said as he walked past her.

He scrubbed a tired hand over his face as he headed upstairs. Brooks was right, something he already knew. He simply couldn't imagine letting Lucy go after all this was settled. And he was going to make damn sure things did get settled, that she walked away as unscathed as possible.

When he stepped into the room, to his surprise, she was sitting up in bed looking half awake. The sleepy, sensual smile she gave him rocked him to his core. "I woke up and you were gone." Disappointment laced her words.

"Couldn't sleep," he murmured, shutting the door behind him.

"Since we both can't sleep, how about we find a way to pass time?" Smiling wickedly, she pushed the covers off to reveal her naked, delectable body.

Hell yeah. He was on board with that.

* * *

"This is it," Skye said, picking up her ringing phone. The number said "unknown" but she had no doubt who it was. Because only one person had the number to this burner phone.

John Leroux.

"You're going to pay for taking my stuff," a very angry male voice said over the line, his accent slightly French Creole.

Skye used a voice distorter to respond. "Yeah, yeah. Let's cut through the crap. I have something you want. And you're going to get something for me. I need to know where Broussard is keeping the women he traffics."

There was a long pause. "Do you know who he works for?"

She stretched out on the couch, kicking her feet up on the ottoman in front of her as she half-smiled at Colt, who was watching her intently. "I do."

"I don't deal in trafficking people," Leroux spat out as if disgusted.

"I know you don't. But you do business with someone who does. Which makes you just as disgusting."

"Fuck you. You know who his boss is. I have no choice but to work with him." There was a hint of fear woven in with his underlying rage.

"You always have a choice but that is neither here nor there. I want the address."

"I wanted a pony for my twelfth birthday party. But we don't always get what we want."

"You're a smart, resourceful man. If you try hard enough to get what I need, I have faith in you. If you don't, all that fine art I took is going to go up in flames. And I'm going to record it burning so you can see it. Then I'll upload the video to YouTube. I imagine a lot of very wealthy, scary people will be pissed if you lose their stuff. Not only lose it, but destroy it. Use that as your motivation to find the address."

"You're insane," he said. "He'll kill me if he finds out I'm involved in anything against him."

"That may be so. You're still going to get what I want. And don't even try any bullshit like trying to meet in person. You get me what I want and you get your stuff back. I'll give you an address where your belongings are being stored. You have no room to negotiate right now so please save us both the time and energy." When he tried to cut in, she continued. "Did you hear about a massacre on Magnolia Street?" she asked, abruptly changing topics.

"Yeah," he said.

"That was my crew. We all walked away unscathed and his guys are all dead. You know who they worked for. Now find me what I want." She hung up.

Colt stood by the fireplace in the living room, watching her with heat in his gaze. "I love it when you get all bossy and threatening," he murmured.

She let out a startled laugh. "Did that seriously just turn you on?"

He nodded. "Hell yeah."

"You guys, I'm *right* here," Gage muttered to the two of them as he worked on his laptop a few feet away from Skye on the same couch.

Colt just shrugged and lifted an eyebrow at her. His expression said, *Do we have time to go upstairs and knock one out?*

Oh, how she wanted to say yes. But she was ninety-nine percent sure they didn't have time to do anything because Leroux was very motivated right now. "I bet twenty bucks he gets us that address within the hour," she said.

"Half an hour," Gage said, without looking up.

"I'm going with forty," Colt said. "And if I win, you get to do that thing I love—"

"Seriously, guys," Gage muttered, amusement in his voice. "Not appropriate for work."

"Yeah, well neither is tossing grenades at people, but I think we're doing all right. If you have a problem though, take it up with HR."

He just laughed before he abruptly sat up. "I might have gotten a hit on one of the women Maria told us about. Her face came up on one of my facial recognition scans on a CCTV. I lost her, but I can narrow down her potential vicinity even more now. To a one-mile radius."

"Good job," Colt murmured at the same time Skye said the same.

She shoved up from the couch, unable to get over the feeling of a ticking clock. The longer the women weren't located, the higher the chance they got caught up in a shitstorm when the Feds brought Kuznetsov down.

Unfortunately, Skye knew from experience that they would very likely end up collateral damage.

CHAPTER TWENTY-ONE

—As long as I have her, I can live with my decisions.—

Leighton grabbed the comforter, tugging it over Lucy as the bedroom door opened.

"Sorry, should have knocked." Colt looked away even though she was covered. "It's time to go. Now. Be in the foyer in five minutes."

Hell. That meant they'd found the place the women were being held. It was just four in the morning, which was good timing. People let their guard down during the early hours of the morning, even if they were guarding something. It was simple human nature.

He turned to Lucy. "I'm sorry—"

"Go. Just stay safe." Lucy gave him a quick kiss, worry in her gaze.

"If something happens to me, you'll be taken care of. I've already talked to Gage," he said, grabbing clothes and gear from his bag. "If for some reason the Feds drop the ball and your uncle goes free, my people will help you disappear if I don't come back."

"Leighton—"

He shook his head sharply. "I don't want to talk about it. Just know you'll be okay."

Sighing, she gave him a look with too many mixed emotions as he hurriedly dressed. "Just come back to me."

"Oh I plan to." But he knew that plans didn't always work out the way they should. He gave her a hard, dominating kiss before grabbing the rest of his weapons and hurrying out the door. He hated leaving her like this, but there was no choice.

Time was of the essence now that they had a location. They needed to move in fast and efficient.

* * *

"Here's the rundown." Colt turned around from the passenger seat while Skye drove in silence.

Leighton and Savage were with them while the others were in another vehicle. They'd chosen nondescript minivans with stickers of families on the back for both of their getaway vehicles. Colt's dad and Nova were currently setting up extra getaway vehicles in the near vicinity of the op in case things got hot.

"Leroux got back to us, and he doesn't get his art unless he's telling the truth," Colt continued.

"He could be setting us up," Savage murmured.

"I know that. But the address he gave is in the same mile radius that Gage narrowed the place down to. It fits."

"Lethal force?" Leighton asked. He knew it was a distinct possibility. Hell, probability. But there were civilians inside so they had to be careful. This wasn't like the last takedown.

"Lethal force if necessary. But I want to leave as many of them as possible tied up for the Feds."

The plan was to go in, disarm the men and free the women. But if there were children there, Leighton didn't care about disarming them; he would kill every single one of those bastards. Hell, he wanted to kill them all anyway and wasn't sure what that said about him.

But he was tired of living in a world where there was so much shit. There was so much garbage every day, and his friends and Lucy felt like the only good in it. He knew that was wrong of course. But it was hard not to get caught up in the bullshit.

"I say we just kill them all," Savage muttered.

Leighton simply grunted in agreement.

Colt gave them a sharp look. "We don't know if the Feds will need them to testify against Kuznetsov."

"Who says they'll testify?" Leighton murmured.

Colt lifted a shoulder. "They're going to jail for what they've done. We'll make sure of it. But if the Feds need these guys to build a stronger case against Kuznetsov, I say we give it to them."

"Whoever's there will be prepared this time." Especially after what had happened on Magnolia Street.

Colt nodded, going silent at that.

It didn't take long to find the house, though they didn't park in front of it, but blocks away in a church parking lot.

Just as they had last night, they surrounded the place and prepared to infiltrate. Only today they had double numbers so they moved inside in pairs. Leighton's partner was Brooks and their entry point was the back door. Even though originally Brooks hadn't planned to take part, he'd refused to sit back while they all went in since Axel wasn't at maximum capacity. He was still here, but providing backup outside, letting them know if they needed to scatter.

On the same count, they all infiltrated the house when Gage cut the power.

With NVGs on, Leighton went in high while Brooks moved in low.

A shirtless man reached for a pistol on the kitchen table but Leighton shot his arm. Even if he would have preferred shooting him right in the face.

The guy cried out but Leighton was on him fast, slamming his fist against his jaw as the man bled.

The man dropped to the floor, moaning even as Brooks took down and disarmed the other one by the refrigerator.

Both men were shirtless, armed, and wearing loose jogging pants—and covered in tattoos that spoke of local gang involvement.

"We've got a situation," Gage said quietly. "Downstairs hallway, man has a knife to a woman's throat. He's not going to let her go. Skye's trying to talk him down.

He only has a visual on her." Gage's voice was quiet through the comm line.

"What side of the house?" Leighton asked.

"East."

Leighton and the others knew the layout of the house thanks to Gage's hacking skills, so he knew exactly where that was. "I'll take him from the window if possible." He just hoped he got there in time.

"Move fast," he murmured.

"Put the gun down and you walk away from this." Skye's low-pitched voice came over the comm line just then.

"I'm not fucking stupid," the man spat as Leighton headed out the back door.

Brooks nodded at him once and motioned that he was going deeper into the house.

Leighton could hear the others taking people down on the second floor—and news that half a dozen women were now safe—but right now his main focus was on saving that girl. They didn't come here tonight to lose anyone. All these women were walking away unscathed. He moved around the edge of the house as Skye continued to talk in the calmest voice he'd ever heard from her. She was almost soothing.

"We're not killing anyone here today," she said.

"You're not cops. And you're not Feds," the man said, his voice rising. "Otherwise you wouldn't be wearing masks! Who are you with? The Mexicans?"

"We're not with any cartels. Or any rival gangs. Put the weapon down and no one gets hurt. So far we've only restrained everyone."

"Shut the fuck up! Who are you?"

"We're CIA," Skye said suddenly, her tone a little sharper now. "And there's only one way you're getting out of this alive. If you're useful."

Leighton wondered where the hell she was going with this line of lies, but mostly tuned it out as she started spinning the guy a bullshit story about how they wanted to turn these guys against their boss. How they needed leverage right now, blah, blah, blah.

Leighton came upon the small bathroom window and started to hoist himself up. The window was frosted so he couldn't take a shot even if he wanted.

There was a shout of commotion.

"The guy's dragged her into the bathroom and barricaded himself in," Gage snapped.

"I'm in place." Leighton plastered himself up against the wall, waiting for a long moment.

"No!" a woman screamed, and he tensed. Then it was silent.

"Stay out!" the man shouted, his words clear through the window. "I just need to think."

A second later, someone inside opened the window. Lifting his weapon, Leighton knew there was only one option for this. He had to take this guy out before he hurt the woman.

There would only be one chance. The window was too high up off the ground for Leighton to get a good hold of him and drag him out. He couldn't risk the woman's life. If she was even alive.

Leighton shut that thought down and focused on the moment.

The man slowly eased his head out, looking left before starting to turn toward Leighton.

He took the shot. "Man down."

The door burst open as the man's body slumped over the windowsill.

"She's alive." Relief filled Skye's voice over the comm. "Bruised up, but alive."

"I'm moving in. Everyone check in," Leighton said. He'd been so focused on taking this guy down he wasn't sure where everyone else was at this point.

Everyone checked in that they were alive and that there'd been only one other casualty—not one of the women—and that all the women were alive and accounted for.

It took a few minutes of talking to the women, some of whom they'd had to translate for, to discover that only one man was missing from the usual crew who watched them. Marco Broussard.

Fucker.

And that none of them had been sent out tonight because of what had happened last night. The women didn't know much, just that the bosses of the men here had wanted to lie low.

As Leighton finished helping drag the men into the living room—where they were dumped facedown with their hands and legs restrained—his burner phone buzzed.

Normally for an op, they went dark, but with so many of their people back at the safe house, they'd all opted to carry burners in case of an emergency.

"Yeah?" he murmured, stepping out of the living room.

"Hey, it's me," Nova said agitatedly. "Lucy's inside The Sapphire. Senior is with her. Her friend is in trouble...and I think she might be too."

CHAPTER TWENTY-TWO

—You know that little voice in your head that says
"Punch him in the dick"? Listen to it.—

One hour earlier

Lucy couldn't go back to sleep after Leighton's abrupt departure. No way could she rest well—or at all—while worrying about him, so she took the world's fastest shower before dressing in jeans and a comfortable sweater. Not her normal go-to wear but she was all about comfort right now.

Downstairs, she nearly backed out of the kitchen when she saw a woman sitting there, drinking coffee, but knew that would be beyond rude. She just wasn't up for a lot of conversation.

The woman, who she'd seen but hadn't been introduced to, gave her a smile. "Hi. You're Lucy, right? I'm Darcy, Brooks's wife."

"Yes, it's nice to meet you." Lucy smiled as she stepped into the room. Immediately she headed for the coffee pot. "Though that seems weird to say, considering the circumstances."

The other woman laughed lightly. "I know, right? Hadley and I flew in to surprise our men and of course they run right into danger as soon as we get here."

"So...you don't have, like, military training or any-thing?" Lucy asked, sitting across from the pretty bru-nette. Because she knew Skye did, and she was fairly certain Nova had some sort of training as well.

Darcy blinked then let out a loud laugh. "Not just no, but hell no. I'm a wedding planner. I have combat train-ing if you consider the bridezillas I deal with, but that's about it."

Lucy found herself smiling despite the worry winding its way through her system. "This feels like an obvious question, but don't you worry about your husband all the time?"

"Oh yeah. When he's off doing whatever they do, yes. I try to block it out, and staying busy with work—which I love—helps."

Lucy looked down at her coffee, not sure if she felt worse or better.

Darcy continued. "I wish I could say it gets easier but...it doesn't. Not really. But they're very trained. In-cluding Leighton, which I'm sure you already know."

She gave a grateful smile to the other woman who was clearly going out of her way to make Lucy feel bet-ter. "He told me a little bit about what he did before, but it helps to hear that he's trained. I'm still scared for him." The fear was wearing away at her.

Two other women walked into the kitchen at that moment. She'd met both of them, albeit briefly, and smiled politely.

Nova and Hadley both returned her smile and practically raced each other for the coffee pot. Nova beat Hadley by a second and gave an evil cackle as she started the Keurig machine. "Don't get in the way of me and my coffee or I *will* shed blood."

"That's mean, woman. My man was just shot. I feel like you should be a little nicer."

"He was barely grazed," Nova said teasingly even as she wrapped an arm around the other woman's shoulders. "And I heard you two going at it a couple hours ago, so I'm pretty sure he's gonna live."

"Gah! You heard us?"

Now Nova dissolved into laughter. "No, but you just admitted that you two were getting busy. Which makes your claim even sadder. If your man can handle sex, you get no special treatment." She picked up her mug with a grin.

"You're sneaky," Hadley muttered, a smile tugging at her lips.

It was clear these women had a good relationship, and Lucy found herself almost envious of it. Because of the way she'd been raised, she didn't have many girlfriends. Sure, she was friendly with most of the staff, but because of her position it was impossible to be actual friends with people you might have to fire one day. She'd always felt like she missed out on having a best friend growing up, and right now only drove the point home.

She wondered if it was weird to hope that one day she'd be friends with these women. Real friends. Then she shoved the thought away as something ludicrous.

Despite what Leighton said to her, Lucy was a realist. She wasn't thinking about the future with him. It would hurt too much to imagine a future where he wasn't in it.

So she wasn't going to.

Before her thoughts could get too self-pitying, Senior strode into the kitchen fully dressed and looking fully awake. Damn. She felt as if she was barely functioning but he looked ready to take on an army.

"You didn't get enough coffee earlier?" Senior's tone was dry as he looked at Nova.

She lifted a shoulder. "Never."

Shaking his head, Senior stepped fully into the kitchen. "I'm sick of takeout. I can whip us all up some omelets if you guys are hungry?"

Lucy felt too shy to respond first but the other women all said yes, so she simply nodded.

"That's what I like to see, a man at work in the kitchen," Nova said, grinning at the older man.

Lucy had a feeling she was really going to like Nova.

As the other women talked amongst themselves and Senior started making breakfast, she soaked it all in and tried not to worry about Leighton. Though that was an impossibility. Nothing could stop her mind from working.

It was going a million miles a minute. Her thoughts were consumed with Leighton, and of course her uncle. Did her uncle know about her involvement with these people? Were the Feds really going to arrest him? And would the charges stick? That was the main thing. So

much was up in the air right now and she had no answers.

Shaking herself out of her thoughts, she nearly
jumped when her phone buzzed in her jeans pocket, indicating a text. She'd only brought it downstairs in case
Leighton contacted her.

She didn't recognize the number but clicked on the
link.

Her chest tightened when she saw Nathan tied to a
chair, one eye swollen shut, his head lolled to the side.
Blood crusted the side of his mouth as he breathed in and
out.

There was a timestamp on the video, and she recognized some of the labeled boxes. He was being held at the
casino.

"Oh my God," she said aloud before she could stop
herself.

Another text came through almost immediately after
the video. *I have a proposition for you. Meet me at the casino
in storage room 6C within twenty minutes or your friend dies.
If you involve the cops, your friend dies. If you bring anyone
with you, your friend dies.*

With shaking fingers, she tried calling the number
but it went straight to a generic voicemail. It was likely
one of those TracFones.

"What's wrong?" Darcy asked.

That was when she realized all of them were staring
at her.

She slid off her stool and stood up. She felt almost
numb. "My friend has been kidnapped. And roughed up.

Maybe tortured. He's at the casino." She held out her phone and Senior grabbed it before anyone else could.

He frowned even as she was already reaching for it.

"I don't care what you say, I'm going," she snapped, preparing for an argument.

Her phone buzzed again. *Remember, if you call the cops, I put a bullet in his head, princess.*

Ice cut through her as she shoved her phone in her back pocket. Only one person called her princess. Marco. Now he had a "proposition" for her? What the hell was that about?

"You can't stop me from going," she said again, looking at Senior now. "I think I know who has my friend."

"Not gonna stop you. But you're not going alone," Senior said, rounding the center island. "And we're not going unarmed. And you're definitely not going looking like you are now."

Surprised by his reaction, she blinked. "You're not going to fight me?"

"I have a feeling you're not staying here unless I tie you up, and I'm not keen on that idea.

"Good, because I'm not letting my friend die. But I know that hotel a heck of a lot better than he does," she said. "I think the man who took him is someone who works for my uncle. He's the only one who calls me princess. He doesn't work at the hotel but he has a lot of access there."

Senior nodded as he took her arm gently. "Come on, we need to get you in disguise so he won't recognize you on any security cameras."

"Oh, that's a good idea." A great one, actually. "Look, I recognize that room Nathan is being held in. It's not the storage room he told me to go to. So if he wants me to go to 6C, we're not going there. We should just go to where Nathan's being held then call the cops."

Senior nodded even as he pulled a gun out of one of the kitchen drawers on their way out.

She blinked in surprise. *What the hell?* They stored their guns in the kitchen? Whatever—she'd contemplate that insanity later.

Nova tried to stop them from leaving, but eventually decided on joining them when she couldn't get ahold of Gage.

Lucy didn't want to be doing this, but there was no way in hell she was just going to sit back and do nothing while her friend was murdered. And she couldn't risk calling the cops. Because Marco would see the police coming a mile away. They would have to follow a certain protocol. And Nathan would end up dead.

Nope. That wasn't going to be on her conscience.

* * *

"Your uncle could be there too," Senior said as the three of them approached The Sapphire barely fifteen minutes later.

Lucy had worked on her disguise on the way, putting on a platinum blonde wig, fake reading glasses, and a sweatshirt with a pink sequined flamingo on the front.

The thing was ridiculous but Nova said it was good as part of her cover.

Since Lucy had no experience with this kind of thing, she was taking Nova's advice.

Her phone dinged again. *Tick. Tock. Time's almost up, princess.*

She swallowed hard, reading the text. "He's texted me again."

"He won't hurt your friend. Not yet. Text him back, tell him you're caught in traffic. He has no idea where you are right now," Nova said calmly from the front seat even as she made another phone call.

No doubt to Gage, who she kept trying to call.

Lucy did as she said, texting back, hoping her franticness came through in a freaking text. Nathan couldn't die. He simply couldn't. She wouldn't forgive herself if that happened.

Tick, tock was the only response she got.

Nausea rose inside her but she ruthlessly shoved it down as Senior turned into the employee section of the parking lot. Wordlessly, she handed him a master keycard.

Senior swiped it over the keypad and the arm lifted, allowing them inside.

The keycard wasn't linked to her specifically, but "management." Still, she had a feeling Marco would be watching for her. If it *was* Marco, and if he was working with someone in security. And at this point, she couldn't rule any possibility out, but she was operating on the thought that it was Marco.

COVERT GAMES | 241

"Go to the second floor," she directed. "We're going to use the employee entrance there, then take the closest service elevator to the third floor. It's actually on the same level with the lobby. Some of the service elevators have cameras—most do, actually—but not all of them. Anyway, we'll be in a private hallway that leads to where I'm supposed to go."

"Are there stairs?" Senior asked.

"Yeah."

"I'll take the stairs so we're not traveling together."

"I only have this one keycard. You won't be able to move around freely."

The older man frowned, but didn't respond as he pulled into a parking spot. "Nova, sit tight. Call the cops in five minutes."

"What?" Lucy demanded.

"Look. The police definitely have their purpose. Right now we have no other backup. The cops need to be called no matter what. Nova has Marco's name and description. She's using a burner and she'll tell them he's waving a gun around the casino. So even if he kills us, he's not getting out of here alive."

Lucy couldn't very well waste time and argue with them. And it wouldn't matter anyway because she was pretty certain they'd just do what they wanted regardless. "Fine. Let's go."

Tick, tock, tick, tock. She could hear the damn clock ticking down in her head.

Heart pounding, she hurried across the half-full parking lot with Senior.

The man might be older, but he was in better shape than her, moving like an athlete as they reached the elevator. He wore a ball cap and kept his head angled down to avoid any potential cameras. Luckily she knew where all the cameras were, so they shouldn't have a problem. Not until they reached the employee-only hallway. Then...they'd just have to wing it. At least she had on a disguise so it was very likely that if Marco was working with someone in security, he wouldn't recognize her.

Not at first anyway.

She swiped the card against the reader, then wiped her damp palms against her jeans.

"Breathe," Senior murmured. "Steady breaths will keep your oxygen flowing evenly. You need to keep a level head." He didn't even look at her as he spoke, just calmly stepped onto the elevator.

God, she wished she could be so cool and collected.

"And remember, he's not going to do anything too stupid while he's here."

"Maybe," she muttered. He'd clearly hurt Nathan at the casino. She felt sick again and suddenly she was glad that Nova would be calling the cops.

When they reached the right level, she took that steadying breath and stepped out with Senior. Almost immediately she saw Carlos, one of the maintenance guys, carrying a small ladder, walking in their direction.

Instinctively, she almost called out a friendly greeting, but then remembered her disguise. So she kept her eyes straight forward and acted like she knew where she was going.

"Three doors down is where I saw him being held," she murmured to Senior even as they passed a woman she recognized who worked at one of the restaurants.

The woman didn't even look up from her phone as she walked by, completely in her own world.

"Right here," she murmured.

"How many cameras are on us?" He didn't look up as he asked.

"A couple."

Senior let out a frustrated sound, but reached for his weapon, which was tucked under his shirt. "No way around it," he told her before opening the door. She knew he didn't want her with him, but she couldn't send this man, this stranger, in there alone.

She pulled up short next to Senior, who had his pistol drawn and was sweeping the mostly empty room. Mostly empty except for Nathan.

Who was leaning against one of the storage bins, his cell phone in hand.

"Lucy!" Nathan stared at her in shock, his one eye widening. The other was red and purple and the swelling looked worse.

"You got free," she rasped out, relief threatening to flood her system. She started to move toward him, but Senior shot out his free hand, nearly clotheslining her as he stopped her.

"I'm sorry," Nathan said, shame filling his blue eyes.

That was when it registered that…he *hadn't* gotten free. He must have never been a prisoner in the first place. *Oh, God.* "But…your face."

"It had to look real," he murmured. "It's not personal."

Not personal? Was he kidding?

"We need to get out of here," Senior murmured. "Toss your phone over here," he ordered Nathan, his weapon still trained on him.

He'd given Lucy a gun too, but she didn't plan to use it—didn't want to touch it.

Nathan threw his phone on the ground even as Senior started pushing her back toward the door.

Lucy froze when she felt the cold steel of a gun at her neck.

Icy talons raked down her spine, freezing her in place.

"I like the blonde wig, princess." Marco's evil voice made her skin crawl. "Don't even think about it," he snapped when Senior started to turn. "Drop your weapon. Now, old man."

Senior paused but let the weapon clatter to the floor.

Bins filled with various decorations they used around the casino filled the room, pressed up against the walls in neat little stacks. But there was nowhere to run, nowhere to hide.

A hard hand gripped the front of her neck as Marco pulled her back to his chest. That was when she felt his erection—and nearly lost it. He must have felt her gun because he pulled it out quickly, leaving her unarmed.

"Tie up the old man for now," Marco snapped out to Nathan, who jumped to it when ordered. "Your uncle couldn't even be bothered to kill you himself," Marco murmured in her ear, his words like an oily film dripping down her spine.

She suppressed a shudder. "My uncle sent you?"

"He told me to get rid of you, to make it look like an accident. For once, I'm not following orders. Because I'm going to enjoy you first. You've always thought you were too good for me." He yanked her even closer now, wrapping an arm around her from behind and grabbing her breast hard.

She cried out in pain, unable to stop the sound.

Nathan looked over from where he was pulling a zip tie around Senior's wrists, his eyes widening. "You...didn't say anything about this. You said you were just going to kill her. Not hurt her."

Oh, so that made it okay. Asshole. She couldn't believe she'd thought Nathan was her friend. He'd always been flighty and self-absorbed, but this...was insane.

Marco moved slightly behind her. There was a rustling sound then he tossed something at Nathan. A big bag of...ah, cocaine. Nathan jumped on it like a junkie, snatching it up and shoving it in his pocket.

"Get out of here and tell security there's no problem down here. We'll be gone by the time they get the cameras back up and running."

"Yeah, yeah," Nathan muttered, hurrying out the door without looking at Lucy. He kept his eyes cast down as if he was ashamed.

Good. If she got out of this, she was... Hell, she just hoped she and Senior got out of this. "You disabled the cameras?" she asked, hoping to keep Marco talking for at least a little bit. If he was talking, he wouldn't be hurting her. Or killing them. She hoped.

Ignoring her question, he dragged her over to Senior, who was zip-tied to one of the shelving rails, and kept his own gun up. "Who do you work for?"

"DEA," Senior said without missing a beat.

And if Lucy didn't know he was lying, she'd have believed him.

Marco whipped her around so fast, she tripped over her own feet. But he yanked her up by the throat, holding her in place as she struggled.

"Tell me the truth or I bend her over and rape her right in front of you." Marco's voice was cold, merciless, and she knew he'd do it if he thought Senior was lying.

No, he'd do it no matter what. That truth registered as her windpipe closed. She clawed and kicked at Marco, but he didn't flinch. He was so strong.

Black spots danced in front of her vision as Senior yanked on his bindings.

"You're killing her," Senior ground out.

"Yep. Tell me who you work for."

"FBI. We're bringing your boss down tonight."

The grip on Lucy's throat loosened, but not by much. Sucking in a breath, she tried to jerk away from him, but he yanked her to him again, wrapping his arm around her throat this time as he held her close.

She felt wetness on her cheeks and realized she was crying. Her entire body felt numb, so she wasn't sure how that was even possible.

"We know about the Feds," Marco snarled. "But I don't think you're with them. The Feds would never bring a civilian into something like this. So that leaves a few options." Suddenly, he shoved her away from him.

Lucy turned, elation punching through her even though she wasn't free at all. But she was glad he wasn't touching her anymore.

"Take your sweater off," Marco snapped, his gaze on her now, his eyes bright with something she didn't want to think about.

"What?"

"Sweater. Off."

She wanted to say no, wanted to fight him, but knew that was likely to get her killed. Oh God, now she was *really* glad that Nova would have called the police. She just hoped they got here in time.

With trembling hands, she did as he said, lifting her sweater up and off. She clutched it in her fingers, holding it tightly at her side as Marco stared at her, his lecherous gaze sweeping over her as if he was imagining...things she didn't want to think about.

"You're definitely not a Fed," Marco murmured, more to himself. "Because you don't have any backup." He paused at a buzzing sound. Then he pulled his phone out of his pocket—but his gun hand didn't waver. He read something, cursed.

When he looked at Lucy, that gleam was back. "I'll be leaving on a trip with your uncle very soon. Yes, he knows about the Feds. And they're stupid enough to believe someone in his organization turned on him. So while they're raiding his home, he'll be long gone on his yacht." His phone buzzed again, but he ignored it. "It's only a shame I won't have more time with you. Now take your pants off."

She blinked at the suddenness of his order, at the brutal gleam in his eyes. He was going to rape her, then kill her right here. "No."

"Take. Them. Off."

"No." If he wanted them off, he'd have to take them off himself.

He took a step toward her, then paused and swung his gun at Senior. "Do it or I kill him now."

"Let him shoot me!" Senior struggled against his bonds, cursing and pulling at the entire shelf.

Tears blurred her vision as she reached for the button of her jeans. She wanted to fight him, but she couldn't let him kill Senior. Oh, she was certain he was going to do it, but if she could just hold out—

Out of the corner of her eye, she saw the door opening slowly. She couldn't see who was entering, but they were moving methodically.

It was Leighton!

By sheer force of will she didn't know she had, she didn't look at him. And she prayed that hope didn't show in her eyes.

Senior continued struggling, shouting now at how Marco was a "pathetic motherfucker."

Marco didn't take his gaze off her, however.

Even though she hated to do it, instead of shoving her pants down, she made a move for her bra instead. She needed all of Marco's attention on her. And there was one surefire way to do that.

As she whipped her bra off, his eyes widened and he rubbed a hand over his crotch. When he did, everything else seemed to move in slow motion.

Leighton pounced like a lion, taking him down with a savage cry. The sound reverberated through the storage room as the two men hit the ground with a violent thud. Marco's gun flew across the room and under one of the shelves.

Clutching her sweater to her, Lucy raced for it, trying to grab it, but couldn't reach it.

"Knife in my back pocket," Senior snapped out.

She grabbed it and cut him free as the two men continued to savagely beat on each other.

Senior shoved her back as they fought. She saw his fallen gun at the same time Marco must have.

He lunged for it but Leighton slammed his fist into Marco's back with a resounding crack. Marco cried out in pain, but Leighton wasn't done.

He slammed his fists into Marco over and over until he wasn't moving.

"Son, stop!" Senior finally snapped.

Leighton looked up at them, his eyes almost glazed over as he stared between the two of them.

"Leighton?" she whispered.

At that moment, the door flew open. Two of their security team raced in, led by Nick, weapons up. They stared at all of them.

Nick trained his pistol on Leighton. "On the floor, hands above your head. Lucy, are you okay?" he asked even as Leighton complied. Even Senior raised his hands over his head.

"I'm okay. This man saved my life. Marco tried to kill me. How did you even know I was in here?"

Nick paused, but then lowered his gun. The two men with him did the same. "I didn't. Nathan offered to check down here when some of the cameras went glitchy, but then when I saw him on camera, he was beat to hell. I tried to get him to tell me what was going on, but he blew me off, said he was fine. So we headed down here… Shit." He turned back to one of the men. "Radio Rick and tell him not to let Nathan off the property." He turned back to her, but kept a wary eye on Leighton, who'd stood and was now moving closer to her. "You're sure you're okay?" His gaze swept over her in a clinical fashion, and she inwardly cursed.

"Yes. Can you…turn around?"

He and the men with him did, and so did Senior, thankfully. Leighton moved lightning fast, grabbing her bra from the ground. She slipped it on with trembling fingers, thankful when he helped her get her sweater slipped over her head.

"I'm dressed," she rasped out, grateful when Leighton slipped an arm around her shoulders.

She wrapped her arm around him, holding on to him for support, and so damn glad he was okay. She wanted to know how he'd known she was in this room, but held off with any questions.

"What the hell is going on?" Nick asked as he turned around.

Marco started moaning on the ground, though she wasn't sure how that was even possible.

Before she could respond, Leighton motioned toward Marco. "He needs to be restrained. Are you going to shoot me if I move to grab those zip ties?"

Nick shook his head as Leighton jumped into action. As he moved, she watched as he stealthily snagged Marco's phone and pocketed it.

"I wish I could tell you what's going on." Lucy decided to go with a partial truth. "I got a text from an unknown number with a video of Nathan restrained and beat up, threatening to kill him if I didn't come here. When I got here, Marco jumped me. He…" Her voice broke and she wasn't faking it. "He was going to rape me."

Nick's expression turned murderous as he glanced down at Marco, and for a moment she thought he might kick the man. Instead, he simply said, "Do you need medical attention?"

"No. He didn't get that far." She shuddered, thinking of what would have happened if not for Leighton.

"Who are you?" Nick asked suddenly, looking at Leighton with a sharp awareness.

"Ms. Carreras's bodyguard. She's had issues with a stalker and I've been keeping an eye on her during off-work hours. The threat escalated, so I came with her to work today and—"

Nick held up a hand when someone tagged him on his radio. He spoke quietly for a few moments, then said, "The cops are here. We're all going to have to talk to them. I need to go meet them."

"Would it be possible to go wait in the employee lounge down the hall? I don't..." Lucy made her voice crack. "I don't want to be near him," she whispered, trembling and turning the waterworks on. Which wasn't too hard, considering she felt as if she was on a wire's edge anyway. More than anything, she wanted to talk to Leighton in private, and she couldn't do that in here.

Nick nodded. "Of course. All of you, come on." He hadn't questioned Senior as to who he was, but she figured that was coming. Either from Nick or the cops. Or both. "I'll keep a guy on the door here, not that I think this piece of trash is going anywhere," he spat, giving Marco a disgusted look.

"I can show them the way," she said to Nick when he started to walk with them. "I know you've got a lot to deal with. Go meet the police."

He looked as if he wanted to argue, but nodded. "I've got my phone on me, but I won't be long."

As they slowly headed down the hallway in the direction of the lounge room, she leaned on Leighton. "Marco said my uncle knows about the Fed raid. He said that he's leaving on his yacht. Soon too. He told me all this because he was going to kill me. He was so smug about knowing what was going on." And he'd been thrilled about planning to rape her, but she left that unsaid because Leighton already knew that much.

Without responding, Leighton pulled out the phone he'd stolen from Marco and opened it up.

"How'd you—"

"Used his thumbprint when I grabbed it," he said quietly, scanning Marco's messages. "And...now I've taken off the login security function."

When his jaw tightened at something he read, she said, "What?"

"Nothing."

"Tell me."

He simply tightened his arm around her, but still wouldn't look at her. Leighton shoved the phone in his pocket. "There's a message from your uncle. You don't need to read it."

"He...really did order Marco to kill me?"

"Yep." He didn't look at her as he pulled his own phone out. He made a call then cursed a moment later. "My Fed friend isn't answering."

"This is the lounge room," she said as they reached an open door. No one was inside, thankfully.

"We're not staying here," Leighton murmured, glancing back down the hallway. A few men were standing together and talking, but no one was paying them any attention. "We'll iron out everything with the cops later but I've got to stop your uncle if what Marco said to you was true."

"This way," Senior said, the first words he'd spoken since they'd left. His wrists were raw, but he didn't seem to be fazed by it at all.

Leighton simply nodded and they headed back the way she and Senior had arrived. She wondered how the hell Leighton had gotten in, but held off asking. There were more important things to worry about. "I can stay—"

"No." Leighton finally looked down at her, his expression hard. "I'm not leaving you. I don't give a fuck what the cops think. You're coming with me. I need—" He cut himself off as they hurried out into the parking garage.

Nova pulled right up to them. "Thank God you guys are okay," she exclaimed as they all jumped in. "I heard the police sirens so I'm assuming...you guys aren't talking to the cops?"

"Where's the yacht docked?" Leighton asked, typing away on his phone and ignoring Nova's question.

Nova didn't seem to care. She just raced out of the parking garage.

"Ah..." Lucy had hoped they'd have a minute to talk or something but knew this was more important. Even if it stung that Leighton seemed so cold and distant. She rattled off the names of two marinas. "He has a couple boats. Both yachts, if you want to get technical. I'm assuming he'd use the bigger one to leave, but I don't know anything at this point."

Leighton's jaw tightened as he looked up both marinas. "Nova, call Gage and give him this info. We're headed to Redwood Wharf. It's closer." Even as he was talking, he tried another phone number. Then cursed.

"Your friend's still not answering?"

"No. They must be moving on him now."

"So what are you planning to do? Stop my uncle yourself?"

"If it comes down to it." He didn't look at her, and she felt something inside her stomach tighten with dread.

Wrapping her arms around herself, she leaned back against the seat and looked out the window at the passing traffic and scenery. It wouldn't take them long to get to the marina.

She just hoped they weren't too late.

CHAPTER TWENTY-THREE

—Life is tough, but so are you.—

"Damn it," Leighton muttered to no one in particular. Hazel wasn't answering her phone—it wasn't even ringing. Which meant she'd definitely gone dark and the op was in play. Well, if Marco was right, the Feds were at the wrong place.

When his phone rang, he answered it immediately. "Yeah?"

"There's a team of Feds here," Gage said quietly. "They must know about his yachts."

"Get out of there. I'll let you know what we find," he said as Nova made another turn. He just hoped there were Feds at Redwood Wharf too. Then they wouldn't have to deal with Kuznetsov and he could get Lucy somewhere safe and take care of her.

"What happened with the house this morning?" Lucy asked quietly.

That was when he realized he hadn't told her anything. He'd been so consumed with getting to her, then stopping Marco. It was a miracle he hadn't killed him. When he'd walked into that room and seen—

Nope.

He had to lock that down *now*. God, she must think he was a monster. He barely remembered what had happened. But he knew he'd been ready to kill Marco with his bare hands. He flexed his fingers at that. His hands were sore from earlier and little flecks of blood had dried on his knuckles. He filed that under shit he'd deal with later. "The women are safe. The men who'd been watching them are contained." He left out the part about two of them being killed. "And an anonymous call was made to the FBI. Last I heard, they moved in and are doing what they do."

"Good," she whispered, turning away from him again.

He wanted to reach out to her, to comfort her, but he wasn't sure if she'd welcome his touch. And right now wasn't the time to push her. She'd just been through a hell of a lot.

"This place looks deserted," Nova murmured as she steered them into a gravel parking lot.

He leaned forward, scanning the parking lot. There were a total of ten vehicles and a bunch of slips. This wasn't a marina so much as a few rows of boat slips.

And the yacht was hard to miss. Huge and sleek with darkly tinted windows. And it was fast. That much Leighton knew. All Kuznetsov would have to do was get to international waters.

"They're close to leaving," Senior said, nodding at a uniformed man running to the boat with a bag in hand.

"Nova, let the others know the Feds aren't here." It was likely that Lucy had only known about this place because of her relationship with her uncle.

There was no way the Feds would have left this place unwatched if they'd known about it.

She was already on her phone as he turned around and grabbed a duffel bag from the back. "Senior, you up for some action?" he asked, unzipping it and pulling out a few extra pistols. Leighton hoped so because he wasn't going in alone. And even though Nova had some training, he couldn't take her along for this one. He simply couldn't.

"You don't even need to ask," the retired Marine said.

"What are you doing?" Lucy asked, staring at them. Eyes wide, she continued before he could think about answering. "He's going to have men with him. And guns! And...just wait for the FBI. This is too dangerous and he's not worth it." She reached for him, and in that moment he knew that he hadn't screwed things up.

Reaching out, he cupped her cheek gently. "I've got to do this. If he gets away, he could switch vessels. Or find any number of ways to evade law enforcement. You'll never be safe if that happens." He leaned forward and kissed her once, gently. "Stay here and keep this." He laid a small pistol on the seat. "Just flip the safety off and fire."

It looked as if she wanted to say more, but she simply nodded. "Be safe," she whispered as he slid out of the vehicle.

"I'll head down the far left dock and loop back up and around to the boat," Senior said. "There's no way to really sneak up on it. We're just going to have to act like we belong here then find a way to board."

"Yeah." And Leighton did not like those odds. "At least this place is pretty empty." There was a thirty-foot catamaran docked a few slips from the yacht and a fishing charter directly across from it. "I'll approach the charter boat, act like I want to rent it."

Senior looked him up and down, frowned. "You look a little rough but it's as good a plan as any."

* * *

"I don't like sitting here," Lucy said as she slid into the front seat next to Nova. She'd kept her wig and the awful sweater on. Mainly because she didn't have anything else to change into.

"Yeah, me neither," Nova muttered, watching the boats just as Lucy was.

"What did Gage say?" Lucy frowned when Leighton moved out of her line of vision for a moment. Then she saw him talking to an older man wearing cargo pants and a T-shirt despite the cooler weather.

Nova tapped her finger against the center console in a staccato pattern. "They're on their way, and they let the Feds know about this place."

Lucy wasn't sure if that made her feel worse or better. It was good the Feds were on the way but what if Leighton got hurt before they arrived? What if Senior did? What if they got more than hurt? She understood exactly how quickly life could change.

God, she couldn't imagine a world without Leighton in it. Since she'd gotten to know him…his haunted eyes had changed. And when he smiled at her? It was as if literal fireworks detonated inside her.

Leighton continued talking to the guy, nodded, then...sort of disappeared. What the hell? It looked as if he'd gone into the guy's boat but now she couldn't see him.

Nova grabbed a pair of binoculars and frowned.

"What do you see?" Lucy asked.

"Nothing. And I don't like this." She kept the binoculars up, sweeping them slowly around.

Each second that ticked by felt like an eternity. Her heart beat loudly in her ears, the *thump thump* overpowering and making her jumpy. Seconds turned into a couple minutes and that felt like an entire eon.

Pop. Pop.

Lucy shifted slightly in her seat at the distant popping sound. "Did you hear that?"

Nova frowned, glancing behind them, then back at the water. "Yeah."

"Was that gunfire?"

A pause. "Maybe."

Lucy jumped out of the vehicle and tucked the small pistol into the back of her jeans. She'd been assaulted and nearly raped today. And Leighton had saved her. She wasn't going to sit on her ass now. Maybe running into this thing made her stupid but she gave exactly zero fucks.

Leighton had changed her life. He was worth this. And it wasn't like she was unarmed.

262 | KATIE REUS

"Lucy," Nova hissed loudly from behind her right before she heard the door close.

She didn't turn around, just walked quickly to the dock. It was interconnected, linking all the boat slips in different rows. As she headed for the row her uncle's yacht was on, she nearly tripped when she saw him jump off the boat onto the dock.

With nowhere to hide, she kept walking, keeping her head down as she pretended to look at her phone. With the wig, she should be disguised enough to get closer.

She watched as he pulled out his own phone and headed in her direction.

Oh, God. This was it. Now or never. She hoped Leighton was okay. And she really hoped Nova stayed back, but she couldn't afford to turn around and look for the other woman.

Reaching behind her, she pulled out the gun and whipped it up.

Uncle Alexei froze, wide-eyed as he registered who she was. "Lucy?" He started to move his free hand behind him.

She flicked the safety off. "Don't do it. I will shoot you."

"Why would you do that?" His voice was deceptively calm, his eyes icy with rage. Not fear, she noted.

But rage.

Well screw him. "How about because you killed my parents?"

He lifted an eyebrow, then simply nodded in a sort of resignation. "Your father was weak. I had no choice. And

I gave you a good life. You had everything you could ever want. You should thank me."

Red blurred her vision for a moment as she stared at this man. This stranger she'd never known who talked so coldly about killing her parents. "I should thank you for letting me grow up without the two people I loved more than anything? Thank you for killing my mama, who never did anything to you?"

Her uncle shook his head slowly, as if in regret. "I didn't want to kill her. But your father had already told her what he was doing, that he'd gone to the Feds. She never would have believed he'd killed himself. I didn't need all the attention that would bring." His words were so matter-of-fact, so devoid of emotion.

"You're a monster!"

He lifted a shoulder. "Some will say that. So, you turned on me? Turned me over to the Feds?"

"You're not as smart as you think," she spat, not willing to tell him anything about the people who'd told her the truth. She desperately wanted to ask about the men inside his yacht, if they'd been hurt, but didn't want to show any weakness. She just needed to keep him here long enough for the Feds to show up. "Where's your security? Because I know Marco isn't coming."

His head tilted to the side slightly. "I'm traveling light for this trip. You killed Marco?"

She swallowed hard.

He snorted. "Of course you didn't. So he must be in jail? He'll never turn on me."

"We'll see."

Sirens sounded far in the distance. They could be a minute away or ten. Sound traveled weird over the water and it was impossible to tell. Sweat beaded down her spine, her hand wavering.

His jaw tightened slightly. "Get out of my way and I won't kill you."

"I'm the one with the gun." Though she could admit she was terrified of using it.

Maybe he saw her fear or maybe he just knew her. He took a step back. Then another one. Then another. "That's what I thought," he murmured. "Too weak."

She moved after him, but she couldn't make herself pull the trigger. He wasn't armed. And...she wasn't sure if she could kill another person even after all he'd done. Her body trembled as he stepped back again, this time toward the other boat. She realized what he must mean to do. Steal the fishing charter.

"Put your fucking gun down now!" A voice boomed through the air as a bleeding, disheveled Leighton jumped down from the yacht.

Her uncle moved fast, whipping out his gun, aiming at the man she was certain she loved.

She didn't think. She pulled the trigger.

And kept firing even as her uncle fell back on the dock, his body splayed at an odd angle.

Blood pooled everywhere as she stared down at him.

Then Leighton was there, taking the gun from her. He said something, but she didn't hear the words. She could see his lips moving, but didn't actually understand him.

"Lucy!" He shook her shoulders once.

She blinked. "Is he…"

"He's dead. Are you okay?"

She nodded. "I thought you were…" She couldn't even say it.

"I shot the controls, took away his method of transportation. Why the hell did you get out of the car?"

Before she could answer, the sound of sirens pierced the air even louder than before. Tires skidded over gravel and then there were voices. So many voices. And people in uniforms rushing toward the docks.

"Stay close to me. We stick together and we don't say a word without our attorney present," Leighton murmured.

"Okay. Where's Nova?"

"Gone. Don't mention her. They're going to cuff us and take us into custody until they can figure things out. Just keep your mouth shut. My friend will make sure we get out of this okay. And our lawyer won't let anything happen to you. No matter what they say. If they tell you I turned on you or some other bullshit, don't talk until your lawyer is present."

Lucy simply nodded and held her hands up as an armed FBI agent rushed at them. She felt numb as she was handcuffed and taken to a vehicle.

Were they going to charge her with her uncle's murder? She wasn't sorry she'd killed him. The only thing she was sorry about was that her cousin would think she'd killed Uncle Alexei without knowing the details. Sweet Liliana would lose both of them if things went south the way Lucy was unfortunately sure they were going to.

Leighton seemed so certain that things would be all right. But…she'd just killed a man.

CHAPTER TWENTY-FOUR

—Fight for the fairy tale. It exists.—

"Jesus, Leighton, you look like shit," Hazel said as she stepped into the pseudo interrogation room.

It was set up as a lounge but Leighton knew better. He jumped up from his chair. "Where is she?" They'd taken his cuffs off a while ago after someone had come in and told him to sit tight and wait for Agent Blake. "I swear to God if she's been charged with anything or injured, I'll burn this whole place to the ground," he snapped out.

Hazel's eyes widened as she took a seat at the little table. "Sit before you give yourself a heart attack."

He crossed his arms over his chest. It had been two hours since he'd seen Lucy. Since he'd seen her hauled off in the back of an FBI car.

"Your girl is fine. Her attorney showed up within minutes—before she'd even had a chance to call anyone or ask for one."

Oh, thank God. Nova or someone had to have called. Maybe Senior. Or just one of the crew. "You charging her with anything? Because it was self-defense. I was right there. He was about to shoot me and she fired."

Hazel nodded again. "I know. That's all she'd tell us. Literally, that's all she's had to say. Her attorney is doing most of the talking. And no, I don't think we're going to charge her with anything. We've got a whole cluster of shit that went down today, including her being attacked at the casino, then leaving the scene of the crime."

"She's a victim."

"I know that. But then she shows up at the marina—one we didn't know Kuznetsov had a boat at."

"Yeah, because the man who attacked and almost raped her told her about it."

"Hell," Hazel muttered, rubbing both hands over her face. "We've got a lot of paperwork to fill out. A. Lot. And you two are both going to have to answer questions. Probably the same ones over and over. But...your girl is fine. And I'll let you see her if you don't go ballistic. All right?"

"I've been the model prisoner."

"You're not a prisoner," she muttered, standing. "And I saw what you did to Broussard's face."

"He deserved it. So you guys taking apart Kuznetsov's operation for good?"

"I sure hope so."

"Is Lucy going to be in danger?"

Hazel paused for a long moment, assessing him. "You really like this woman."

"I more than like her." He loved her. But Lucy was going to be the one who heard that first, not his friend.

Hazel's eyes widened ever so slightly, but then she smiled. "Good. I like her too. She's tough. And no, I don't think she's going to be in any danger. But we've got a shitload of stuff to figure out. It won't be an easy wrap-up of this case."

Yeah well, that wasn't his problem. The only thing he cared about was getting to Lucy, holding her in his arms and making sure she was okay. Then he was going to tell her the truth, that he loved her and couldn't live without her.

* * *

Leighton rarely felt at a loss, but right now he was floundering as Lucy stepped out of the shower. She seemed...not exactly defeated, but she was clearly exhausted and struggling.

She blinked when she saw him waiting there with a fluffy robe he'd found. She had some silky ones but he figured this would be more comfortable for her now. He handed her the little hair twisty thing she used to wrap her wet hair up in and then her towel.

"You don't have to do this," she murmured, a spark of amusement lighting up her pretty blue eyes for the first time since they'd left the Feds' office.

Senior had been there to pick them up and they'd all been mostly silent on the drive back to her condo. He and Nova had been the ones to call in the attorney for Lucy. It was good they hadn't been there when the Feds had shown up, precisely why the two of them had vanished. The local cops still wanted to know who Senior was, according to Hazel, but thankfully Hazel was shutting down that line of questioning. They'd taken Broussard into custody for so many crimes he'd never see the light of day again. He wasn't their problem anymore unless they needed Lucy to testify, but Hazel didn't seem to think she'd need to. Broussard had agreed to cut a deal—not that it would lessen his jail time by much. If any. But he wouldn't be put into a prison with people who wanted to kill him. Something told Leighton that wouldn't matter. Hazel had also told him that a couple local cops were wanted for the murder of Michael Atkins, which could explain the police presence at his house the night Skye and Colt were there. But really, Leighton didn't care about that.

"I want to," Leighton said, holding out the robe after she hung up her towel.

She slipped it on, sighing as she wrapped it around her. "I feel like I could sleep for a thousand years."

"I bet. How are you holding up?" It felt like a stupid question.

She lifted a shoulder. "I…don't know. I need to talk to Liliana but I'm saving that for after I get some sleep. Your friend said they'd want to talk to me again tomorrow. Well, later today I guess."

It was now one in the morning so yeah, technically it was today. "I'll be with you and so will your attorney."

"Thank you again for the attorney. She was a shark. If I hadn't been so shell-shocked I probably would have appreciated her more."

"You don't have to thank me for that."

She lifted a shoulder, then blinked. "Have you eaten or anything? I just realized—"

Cutting her off, he simply pulled her into a hug. "You don't need to worry about anything else but you right now."

"Leighton..." Trailing off, she laid her cheek against his chest.

She never continued, so he just held her close, inhaling the subtle tropical scent of her shampoo and enjoying the feel of her against his body. "One of the guys dropped off some food. Italian, comfort food if you're hungry."

"I didn't think I would be, but I'm kind of starving," she said as she pulled back from him. Then she frowned, as if taking him in for the first time. "Did you change?"

"I took a quick shower earlier." The world's quickest, because he'd wanted to be waiting for her when she got out. "Why don't you do whatever you need to do and I'll get your food ready."

"Thanks... I know you don't want me to say thank you, but I'm saying it anyway. Thank you for all of this. For being here." For a moment she looked as if she wanted to say more, but then she just gave him a small half-smile.

Lucy pulled the towel from her hair after Leighton left, the simple action exhausting her. It didn't take her long to brush her hair and pull it into a loose, damp braid. Getting dressed, however, was another exhausting action. She stared at her closet, hating the very thought of having to make any decisions.

She'd killed her uncle. Actually killed him. Something she was trying to wrap her head around.

She went from feeling hot, to cold. Now she couldn't stop the shivers racking her body so she grabbed a sweater and tugged it on over a pair of yoga pants. She'd been compartmentalizing her sadness her whole life, so right now she did the same. She'd deal with the aftermath of what she'd done later.

When she saw Leighton in her kitchen, a bittersweet feeling pulsed through her. The man was perfect. Sweet and caring—and she needed to give him up. Not today though.

But she couldn't expect him to stick around for all the stuff she'd be dealing with soon enough. He lived in another state, and she'd be picking up her niece soon and becoming a full-time guardian. That was a whole lot to drop on anyone, let alone someone in a new relationship.

"I don't know how your friends knew, but eggplant parm sounds perfect," she said, sitting at the countertop where he'd set out two plates with food piled on. He'd even poured her a glass of wine and had somehow gotten beer for himself. Something else his friends must have brought over.

"Good." He dropped a kiss on top of her head, but didn't pressure her for conversation as they ate, mostly in silence.

He'd also turned on Pandora to an instrumental-only station. She hadn't thought she'd be able to eat so much, but before she realized it she'd demolished everything and was about to fall asleep right in the kitchen.

"Come on, leave the dishes." Leighton guided her out of the room and she didn't have the will to argue. She felt like a puppet, just letting him lead her around.

And she didn't care. Right now, she was okay with him taking care of her. She was going to let it happen.

Hours later Lucy opened her eyes to the feel of Leighton's big, sexy body wrapped around her. His breathing was steady so she assumed he was asleep, but when she went to move, he tightened his grip around her middle.

"How are you feeling?" he murmured against her neck, his voice dropped low and sensual.

"Surprisingly good." She could probably sleep for another few hours, but instead she turned in his arms, instantly meeting his mouth with hers.

She knew she was going to have to let him go so right now she was going to grasp onto this precious moment with him.

In an instant he had her underneath him as he pinned her to the bed with his rock-hard body. His mouth plundered and took what she freely offered.

She arched into him, wrapping around him even as he somehow stripped her expertly and completely. Soon they were both naked and he was pushing inside her slick folds, deep and slow.

She'd never felt so treasured in her life as she did when he took her so completely. She wasn't sure how long they stayed in bed or how long he teased her body as if he'd been doing it forever. After two orgasms for her and one for him, she collapsed against the sheets, her body sated, even if her mind was working overtime.

He pulled her close to him so that she was curled up against the long length of him, her legs thrown over his waist. If she could, she'd stay like this forever.

"Sweetheart?" he murmured, tracing his hand down her spine lazily.

"Hmm?"

"I need to tell you something." There was almost a sense of urgency underlying his words.

Panic exploded inside her as she thought about all the things he might be about to say. At the moment, she didn't think she was capable of dealing with anything. "What about?"

"Us. My feelings for you."

She shifted slightly to look at him. "Can we not talk about anything right now?"

His expression carefully neutral, he simply nodded. "Okay."

She curled back up against him, savoring all his warmth and strength. For now, she just needed to live in the moment. Later, she'd face reality.

CHAPTER TWENTY-FIVE

—I was born to love you.—

Three days later

L ucy stared out the window of her condo, shoving back that little voice in her head telling her she was about to make a mistake.

She wasn't making a mistake. She was doing what had to be done. Even if it carved her up inside.

The dust hadn't exactly settled, but she wasn't scheduled to see the FBI again anytime soon. After having "meetings" with them the last three days straight, she was exhausted. Now she was taking time off work to go get Liliana and bring her back to New Orleans. Though the truth was, she didn't want to work at The Sapphire anymore. She wasn't even sure she wanted to live here anymore. She had too many things up in the air right now, and Leighton didn't deserve to be dragged into the mess of her life.

"Hey, everything okay?" Leighton's voice sounded behind her and she nearly jumped. He'd told her he'd be back, but she hadn't heard him come in.

And the way he asked her, she realized he must have said her name a couple times. "Yes," she said automatically. "I mean..." She looked down at the little bag he had in his hand. "What's that?"

"I got you those pastries you like. I know you've got a lot of stuff to deal with today and thought this might help."

He was definitely making this a lot harder than it had to be. And she hadn't even told him she'd be leaving today. "Thank you," she murmured, taking his other hand and leading them over to the couch. "We need to talk."

He instantly sat, twisting so that he faced her, his knees touching hers. "That doesn't sound good."

She tried to muster a smile but couldn't because she hated everything about this. "Now that we're both free and clear for the most part, when are you going back to Redemption Harbor?" He'd told her a whole lot more about his life, including where he lived, over the last three days, and she loved everything about him. And she hated that she couldn't be with him. But the timing was wrong. Everything was wrong.

"You're trying to get rid of me?"

"No. I just know that you have a life and you can't be stuck here helping take care of me. I've got a handle on all of this and I don't want you to feel obligated—"

"I don't feel obligated. I want to be here. And I'm going to stay as long as you need me."

That was what she was afraid of. The man was honorable and would stick here with her long after he wanted to go. And she wasn't going to let that happen. "I am incredibly grateful for everything you've done for me. *Everything.* I still feel like a giant mess but I'm getting more of a grip on everything. Or I will once all of my uncle's estates and other crap are settled."

A lot of it was being seized by the government but not all of it. Thankfully, her trust and her cousin's trust were completely separate and untouchable, per her very high-priced attorney. But she was letting the lawyers figure out all that crap because she didn't care. She didn't want any of his dirty money anyway. And if she ended up with something from him, she was going to donate it to charity. Or add it to Liliana's trust.

"Where are you headed with this?" he asked quietly, not taking his gaze off her.

"I booked a flight out of here tonight," she said. "I need to get my cousin. She never wanted to go to school over there and right now she needs me. I'm not going to ask you to be in a relationship with me when I'm literally about to become a parent. Not technically, but I'm her guardian, so I'll be a single parent for the next few years. I have so many decisions to make right now regarding her, where we live, my job...everything."

"Why can't I be with you while you figure things out?"

She leaned forward and kissed him gently for a long moment. God, she was going to miss him. "I never want to be something you feel burdened with. And you are sweet enough and honorable enough that you'll stick around even if you're tired of me. Tired of all the responsibility I'm going to have soon. It might sound okay now, but trust me, it'll get old fast.

His expression darkened. "You think I'll get tired of you?"

"I honestly don't know. I just know I'm facing a lot right now and I can't put that burden on you. It's not fair. And the guilt would eat away at me."

"Spell it out, Lucy."

"There can't be an us. I know what you said the other night—"

"I didn't even get to say it," he growled. "You wouldn't let me tell you that I love you."

She clapped a hand over his mouth and shook her head. "Don't say it."

He gently grasped her wrist and dragged it away from his mouth. "Covering my mouth won't change anything. I love you. So you go get your cousin. And when you come back, I'll be waiting for you. I'm not going anywhere."

"Leighton. This is not how breakups work. I'm breaking up with you. I'm ending things. You can go home guilt free. You're officially off the hook now."

He leaned forward and kissed her, long and deep.

She leaned into him, savoring his taste and masculine scent for as long as she could have him. When she pulled back, her heart was beating out of control and her breathing was uneven. "I think you need to go." Because if he kissed her again, she wasn't letting him go. She wasn't that strong.

And she didn't want to be selfish where he was concerned. He didn't deserve to be saddled with all her baggage.

"Tell me you don't love me," he whispered.

She tried to find the words, but couldn't force them out. Couldn't force the lie out. There had been enough lies in her life. But just because she loved him didn't mean they could be together.

He gave her one heated look before he kissed her forehead and stood. "I'm always a phone call away."

Disappointment stabbed deep, cutting right through her chest cavity, that he was giving up so easily. Which told her all she needed to know. She'd done the right thing. Cutting the cord now before she'd fallen too hard... Okay, that was a total lie. She'd already fallen for him. It hurt now and it would hurt even worse later.

She let the tears fall as she heard the door shut behind him. But she only allowed herself to cry for a little while. She had to pack and she had to get her shit together because she was soon going to be Liliana's guardian.

She had to be strong for Liliana. Because her cousin had just lost everything. As awful as her father had been, Alexei had still been her father. Sighing, she swiped the last of the tears and stood.

It was time to face reality.

* * *

Lucy rolled her carry-on behind her, her purse tucked against her shoulder. She'd forgotten how much she hated Heathrow Airport. It was the most congested airport in the world, she was certain. But she'd made it through customs and would soon see her cousin. All the sights, sounds and people were a blur as she passed them. Just streams of noise and color she'd found she was really adept at tuning out.

But soon she'd be face to face with Liliana. Who knew she'd killed Alexei. They'd talked on the phone and FaceTimed and Liliana hadn't been angry at Lucy for what she'd done. She'd...known about her father. Not all of it, but she'd known a lot more than Lucy. She hadn't hated him, but apparently she hadn't loved him either. Something she'd never told Lucy. Right about now, Lucy needed to hug her, to see her in person.

And to take her home.

As she stepped out onto the curb, she looked at the line of waiting cabs and the dreary, overcast sky and sighed. She knew how this worked. The cabs started from the front of the line and you took whatever was available.

She started heading that way, but jerked to a halt when a very familiar, very sexy man stepped in front of her. Looking rested and good enough to eat. She blinked, certain she was seeing things. "What are you...? How did you...?"

"I'm helping a friend in her time of need," Leighton said, giving her a grin that was far too wicked. "I flew over on the company's jet and now I'm taking you to pick up your cousin. And we'll be flying back on the jet as well."

She blinked, staring at him as she tried to find her voice. "We broke up. This is insane."

"Nope. You broke up with me. And I decided to reject that." He said it so matter-of-factly. As if this was all normal.

"You can't reject my breakup."

"Pretty sure I just did. Come on, I've got a waiting car. And I'm pretty sure it's about to rain so unless you want to get soaked..." He moved lightning fast and grabbed her carry-on before she could protest. Not that she really wanted to.

She hurried to keep up with him, knowing exactly what he was doing. He was trying to make this impossible for her to say no to him.

She watched him, all long, lean lines and hard muscle covered up by a sweater and jeans. His clothing did nothing to cover up the predator underneath. The man she'd been having dirty dreams about. The man she'd been missing more than breathing. After putting her carry-on in the trunk of a hired car, he waved the driver off and opened the back seat for her.

Numb and exhausted, she slid in, grateful the seats were heated. And okay, she was grateful he was here now.

"How was your flight?" he asked all casually. As if he hadn't just surprised her in London.

"Honestly I barely remember it. I slept most of the time. I seriously can't believe you're here."

"I can't believe you thought you could get rid of me. If you'd told me you didn't love me, I'd have walked away. But I saw that look in your eye."

The driver pulled away, clearly knowing where he was going. At this point, nothing surprised her about Leighton. He'd known where to pick her up so of course he knew where she was going now.

"Look, if you really don't want a relationship with me, fine. But that doesn't mean we can't be in each other's lives. I love you, and that's not changing. But I also like you. And I don't want to lose your friendship. You need a friend right now. And I can be that person, no strings attached. I don't need anything from you."

"You can't say stuff like that," she whispered.

"But it's true. And I do love you."

"I love you too," she said, not whispering now. "I love you so much. I just don't want to be a burden—"

"Stop with that shit."

"I just want you to know, that you don't have to feel—"

"I'm a big boy," he said.

"You're not a boy."

His lips quirked up. "Fine. I'm a grown man. I can make my own relationship decisions. And you were trying to make them for me. Why the hell would you think I'd let you deal with all this on your own?"

"I have no idea where I'm even going to be living soon! I'm literally living one day at a time as I figure things out. And bringing my cousin back home with me is the first one on my list. After that, I've got to decide if

I want to stay in New Orleans or move. Then, if I move, which I'm pretty sure I'm going to, find a job. Oh, and figure out where Liliana will go to school. Then—"

He kissed her, soundly, and the only reason she pulled back was because they had a driver. It was weird enough the guy could hear their conversation. She wasn't going to have a full-on make-out session with Leighton.

"You're going to figure things out," he murmured, leaning close to her ear. "And I'm going to give you orgasms every night." He spoke so low she could barely hear him, but his words surged straight to her core, making heat blossom between her legs.

"You're very sure this will work," she whispered, pulling back so slightly.

"I am," he said, looking into her eyes. "Because we are meant to be."

There was no way she could argue with that. And she didn't want to. Because she felt the same way. She felt like she'd been made for this man. This wonderful man who'd given her back her parents in a way. Because of him, she knew that her life with them hadn't been a lie.

And now he was offering to be her rock, and she was going to take it. She'd lost so much, and she couldn't bear to lose Leighton.

Not when he'd flown across the ocean for her. No, this was a man worth fighting for.

CHAPTER TWENTY-SIX

—It's never too late to live happily ever after.—

Two months later

"Where's Leighton?" Liliana asked as she stepped into the kitchen, her dark hair mussed as she wiped the sleep from her eyes.

Lucy looked up from her coffee mug. "What do you mean? He won't be over until later." It was Saturday, and he was taking the two of them out to brunch later.

Her cousin snorted. "I know he sneaks out every morning. I'm not stupid."

Lucy winced as she set her mug back down. "You know about that?"

"Oh my God, I'm fourteen. I don't care if you guys are having sex."

Lucy winced again. "I'm new to this whole guardian/parent thing. I just hope you know that it's not casual or anything. That I wouldn't be bringing random guys by or anything—"

"Of course I know that. I also know that man wants to marry you as soon as possible." She pulled down a box of tea bags and picked her favorite, Earl Gray, before putting it into the water-filled pot on the stove.

"What are you talking about?"

"Come on. I know where it's headed with you guys. The way he looks at you is crazy."

She knew that Leighton loved her but marriage seemed kind of soon. They'd just gotten settled into a routine. But... "How would you feel if we do get married?"

Liliana shrugged, having settled very easily into life in Redemption Harbor. Probably because she was finally living with family for the first time in her life. "I really like him. And he treats you well. He's probably one of the nicest men I've actually ever met. He's like this giant teddy bear around you. If you guys get married, I think we should move to a bigger place though. Maybe someplace that has horses," she said, grinning. She'd been spending a lot of time at the Alexander ranch.

It turned out that Brooks was a billionaire cowboy with a huge ranch, and he welcomed anyone he considered family there. Since she was with Leighton, they were now family too. It was...taking some getting used to. Having so many people who cared about her and Liliana with no strings attached was incredible, if overwhelming.

"Anything you want," Lucy said. "But don't think this means that we're getting married. Leighton and I haven't talked about that at all."

"I have a feeling you'll be engaged by spring," her cousin, who was far too young to know about such things, said as she smiled and pulled out her favorite mug. It had dancing unicorns on it to match the ones on her sleep shirt.

Things had gone more smoothly than Lucy expected when she'd moved her cousin back here. Liliana had hated boarding school. Truly, utterly hated it in a way that she'd never told Lucy about. She still kept in touch with some friends, but come to find out she'd always suspected what her father did. Not the depth of it, of course, but she'd had way more of an idea than Lucy ever had of who Alexei had truly been.

Because some of her friends had told her that they'd heard things. And one of her friends had a father in one of the cartels. Which was something Lucy was definitely not going to think about. Liliana had always been too afraid to ask Lucy because she'd been afraid that Lucy was involved in the same things her father was.

Now everything was out in the open, and they'd made a life for themselves. Oh, Lucy was still learning, and figured that the whole parenting thing was going to get harder as Liliana got older. But she loved it in Redemption Harbor.

Living in New Orleans had been an impossibility for her. There had been too many memories there. Marco was in prison—so was Nathan. But they were very small fish compared to the people the Feds had brought down. Agent Blake checked in every now and then to give her updates, and Lucy was very grateful because she knew the woman didn't have to. Lucy was fairly sure she checked in more out of respect for Leighton but it didn't matter. She was grateful for the updates, regardless of why they came.

Hell, she was grateful for her whole life here. Leighton had asked her to move to Redemption Harbor and it had been an easy choice. Starting over with the man she loved? Not a hard decision. Once he'd shown up in London, she'd known without a doubt that he wasn't walking away from her. He was in this for the long haul. And so was she.

* * *

"What are you up to, sneaky man?" Bundled up in a thick coat, scarf, gloves and boots perfect for the January weather, Lucy glanced over at Leighton, who'd decided to take her on a surprise ATV drive on Brooks's property. And it was just the two of them.

Even though Liliana was older than Valencia, the little girl had asked her to come ride horses at the ranch. And since there was no way Liliana would ever say no to her, Lucy and Leighton had some time alone where they could do whatever Leighton had planned.

Ever since Liliana had told her she knew what they were up to a week ago, Lucy had felt weird about having Leighton over.

"You'll see." He glanced at her, his expression unreadable.

"It's pretty cold, so if you're planning to get naked...I'm probably going to leave most of my clothes on."

He let out a startled laugh and reached for her hand as they drove over a dip in the dirt road. "I wasn't planning on that. But if it's on the table, I'm in."

Tightening her grip in his, she pulled in a deep breath of the fresh winter air. She loved it out here and thought that if one day she and Leighton did get married, maybe he'd want to move out here. It was only twenty minutes from the city and from her new job—where she now worked for Mercer Jackson, running one of his new restaurants. And though she loved the condo she and Liliana lived in, there was something to be said about being surrounded by acres of green and trees.

It made her feel at peace in a way she'd never imagined.

"You okay?" he asked quietly, sensing her mood.

As always. "I'm good. Just thinking about how much I love it out here. And how much I love you." She never got tired of saying that.

He simply squeezed her hand tight and continued driving. When he slowed a few minutes later, she shifted slightly in her seat as they pulled up onto...well, she wasn't sure what it was. A cluster of trees had been cut down and a big spread of land had been cleared. And huge framing for a house had been started, but no slab had been poured yet.

"Oh, Brooks is building a new house?" She knew that a bunch of his ranch hands lived on the actual property. And his dad did too.

"This isn't Brooks's land," Leighton said, pulling up to the wooden boards.

"Oh...crap. Should we head back?" She'd assumed Brooks owned all of this area.

290 | KATIE REUS

"We're good." He turned the ignition off and stepped out. "Come on."

"Ah, okay. What is this?" She rounded the ATV and immediately reached for his outstretched hand. She couldn't seem to get enough of touching him, of feeling like she finally belonged somewhere—to someone. She had a real family now. One that wasn't defined by blood only.

Leighton cleared his throat, seeming nervous for the first time in...ever. "I hope it will be our home."

"What?"

"I, ah, I bought this spread of property from Brooks. It's about ten acres and there's a direct shot to the main road, so we won't have to use an easement."

"Um, okay." She wasn't sure what that meant, or what it meant that he'd bought a place out here. When she turned to him, he dropped down on one knee.

She stared at the box in his hand as he swallowed hard. Her confident Leighton, who no longer had sad eyes, looked nervous.

"Yes!" she shouted even though he hadn't actually asked her anything.

He let out a long breath and grinned. "I bought this property and I want to build a house here. One that's new and ours. Something we build together from the ground up. Liliana will be able to have a horse, or more, if she wants. I probably should have asked you first, but—"

"Yes, yes! I want all of this. And you, forever."

Laughing, he opened the box and slipped the sparkly ring on her finger before kissing her hand. Then he tugged her down to him, where he kissed her again. And again, and again.

And despite what she'd said about not getting naked, when he kissed her senseless after offering her everything she'd never known she wanted, she threw out her "no sex outside in the winter" rule. Then she claimed the man she'd fallen head over heels in love with. And let him claim her right back.

Northern Afghanistan

Leighton stared through the scope of his Schmidt and Bender, watching a few civilians step out of their homes, starting the day. Up at this elevation, his balls were freezing, but this mission should be easy enough.

In and out. That was the job. Extract the high-value target, then get back to base just in time for Thanksgiving. The food would still be shitty, but for any holiday, it was ten percent less shitty than usual and he wouldn't be stuck eating an MRE. The turkey would be dry and the mashed potatoes cold, but he'd take it.

"Got any teriyaki left?" asked Hitch, his team member next to him up on the ridge for their part of this mission.

"Yep." He didn't move from his position, slightly shifting his long-range rifle as a man wearing a Peshawari cap and other traditional garb stepped onto a well-worn path headed toward the small building on the outskirts of the village. The building where their HVT was supposed to be hiding.

"So, you gonna share?"

"Nope. You can have some Cajun jerky though." His friend Mary Grace sent him care packages often, which always included beef jerky, and he shared with the guys.

"Stingy," Hitch muttered, no heat in his voice.

Leighton just snorted. "You're greedy."

"True enough. Man, I'm ready to get back to base."

Yeah, no shit. Leighton was ready to get back stateside, not just to base. He was tired of...everything here. Just tired. "Looking forward to your near beer?" he asked dryly, his voice low enough that it wouldn't carry. His breath curled in front of him, a wisp of white smoke barely discernible in the air. In another month or two there'd be snow on the ground, all the greenery from this area covered. That was the thing that had surprised him more than anything when he'd first arrived in Afghanistan—how lush and green some areas were down in the valleys. He'd gotten over that surprise years ago, however.

"Fuck." Hitch let out a muted laugh. "And hell yeah. I'm gonna drink the shit out of mine."

Leighton didn't laugh, even though he wanted to. For Thanksgiving or any holiday, they were given "near beers," bullshit nonalcoholic beers that were piss warm. But it was better than nothing.

"Would you two assholes shut up?" Morris said through their comm line, making both of them snort softly. "I'm getting a fucking hard on thinking about my near beer."

"Jesus Christ, we've been out here too long," Leighton muttered. "And a Rip It would be better." Rip Its were just as bad as the near beers. Discount energy drinks that no one back home had ever heard of.

Hitch grunted. "Fine, you can give me yours."

"Hell no—I see more movement," Leighton said, going still as he watched two more men he'd never seen before walking down that same well-worn path, heading out of town.

Their HVT was a Taliban leader who'd helped kidnap a physicist and her family—forcing her to work for them and using her family's lives as bargaining chips. Like a bad goddamn movie, a small group of Taliban from this region had gotten their hands on uranium from Iran. At least that was the intel the CIA had given Leighton and his team.

So here they were on Thanksgiving Day waiting for the affirmative so the assault team on the ground could go in and extract the guy. Alive. Leighton and Hitch were the air-forward controllers for their MARSOC team and, while he didn't expect much engagement, they were ready to go if necessary.

Once they got the guy back to base, the CIA would take him into custody and do whatever they needed to do to find the physicist's location. Because while they knew she'd been taken and by whom, no one knew *where* she and her family were. And no matter how tough or committed someone was to their cause, ninety-five percent of the time, people cracked under torture. It was simply human nature. Whether the intel gleaned from it was good or not was another story. Not his problem though.

"How many?" Morris asked.

"Two men."

"We're going in now." Morris's voice was clipped.

"We got your six." Leighton watched as two four-man teams moved out of the nearby forest and approached the building. The building was far enough on the outskirts of the small village that no one would be able to see them.

Quiet predators, they crept toward the building, moving in perfect formation as they spanned out. The sun was just peeking over the nearby mountain, giving Leighton and the rest of them enough light to see movement from the nearby village. Intel said this guy was hiding out here, using a few local contacts to communicate with the outside world, but he was basically alone.

As Morris, the team leader, motioned with his hand, the eight men on the ground got in position at the building entrance.

Morris kicked the door in, rushing in with the others. *Pop. Pop... Pop. Pop. Pop.*

Leighton watched as the doorway lit up with gunfire, the flashes one after the other. He listened through the comm as the team faced resistance—and ultimately got what they'd come for.

"Target acquired. Five casualties... There's a stockpile of weapons here," Morris said over the comm. "Way more than we expected."

Five casualties meant the HVT wasn't alone as they'd been told. *Shit.* Leighton shifted again as movement to the right caught his eye. "Tangos headed your way. All armed."

The teams moved out of the house, one man carrying their target. "How many?"

Shouts rose into the morning air as he and Hitch scanned the incoming enemy. "Fifty...maybe sixty. It looks like the whole damn village." This wasn't just some random village Farooqi had been staying at. This had to be some kind of base for these guys.

"Engage," Morris ordered. "Meet at the LZ point."

Hitch had already started firing on individual targets before Morris had finished talking,

Pop. Pop. Pop.

Shouting over the sound of the team's fire, Leighton called in the airstrike even as the target building exploded—someone must have tossed a grenade inside to destroy the weapons. This op was too far from base for artillery fire to reach.

As soon as he'd called in the coordinates, Leighton aimed at his first target. A man carrying an AK-47. Gunfire erupted below them as he zeroed in on the guy's center mass, pulled the trigger. Then racked his weapon again.

Next to him, Hitch did the same.

Thwump. Four feet to his left, dirt kicked up, spraying everywhere.

"Got him," Hitch said.

Leighton watched the shooter holding the long-range rifle fall, then aimed for the man next to him. *Pop.* Target down.

Rinse. Lather. Repeat.

Though it felt like an eternity, maybe ten minutes had passed when, in the distance, he could hear the fighter jets coming in hot.

298 | KATIE REUS

"We're clear!" Morris shouted over the comm. "Pull back now."

Pop. Pop. Leighton and Hitch both fired again before crawling backward, weapons in hand. Once they were clear of firing range, they would have to hike half a mile back to the extraction point. Even as they moved back, he saw the explosion before he heard it.

Smoke and rubble shot high into the air, an outward wave of destruction as part of the village disappeared under the force of the five-hundred pounders. If it had been JDAMs being dropped, the entire town would have been leveled.

Boom. Another one slammed into the side of the mountain, missing its target.

That was their cue to get the hell out of dodge. No one was firing on them anymore as the men below them scattered like ants, running for cover.

Weapons in hand, he and Hitch raced south, heading for the LZ point and their waiting helicopter.

It was time to get the hell out of there.

* * *

"Hey, where were you this morning?" Hitch jogged up out of nowhere as he fell in next to Leighton. They were back on base, far from the op they'd gone on yesterday.

"Woke up early, went running." Instead of joining Hitch for their normal morning workout at the gym, he'd needed some space to clear his head. Running was the only thing that did that.

"What's going on with you?"

"Nothing."

Hitch just shrugged, but didn't say anything. Instead he kept walking with him.

"You going to the chow hall too?" Leighton finally asked.

"Nope. Just following you until you tell me what's wrong. You've been a ghost the last two days."

Leighton didn't want to talk about it. Didn't want to talk about anything. "Just tired, man. Ready to get the hell out of here." *Here* as in Afghanistan. He wanted to be stateside and, even if he couldn't quite voice it yet, he was ready to get out for good. He loved the Marines, but he was done.

"You and me both. So you hear about the HVT offing himself?"

Leighton stilled for only a moment as they stepped inside the chow hall. "No. When did this happen?" They'd just brought the guy in yesterday.

"Dunno. Heard it through the grapevine that someone with the CIA screwed up. Farooqi got an opening and decided to kill himself instead of talk. And...Professor Evans," Hitch whispered, "has been found dead too. Murdered. Her and the whole family."

Leighton didn't respond, just got in line with his friend. He didn't want to eat, his stomach tightening with the news that their last op had been pointless. Well, not pointless. It was all part of the deal. He knew that. But goddamn, he was tired down to his bones of not

300 | KATIE REUS

making a difference. Maybe he was, but lately it didn't feel like it.

"Heard you were asking about the BDA. What did they find?" Hitch asked.

Damn, nothing was a secret over here. He'd asked the leader of the Marine unit that had conducted the bomb damage assessment of the targeted village to see what they'd found. "Nothing unexpected. Destroyed weapons and ammunition." And a lot of dead people. Including children.

One of the pictures he'd seen was seared into his brain. A charred teddy bear with one missing eye. He shook it off, shoved the image away.

He had two months until he got to go home. He needed his head on straight if he wanted to get out of here alive. He couldn't get so caught up in his own head that he got himself killed. Or worse, got some of his guys killed.

The only thing he was sure of now was that it was almost time to get out, to start a different life. Become a civilian for the first time since he was eighteen.

Thank you for reading Covert Games. I really hope you enjoyed the book and the deleted prologue. I went back and forth over whether I should keep it and the readers I polled, including my editors, were split! So I went with my instinct and deleted it, but it shows a bit more insight into Leighton that I thought you guys would love so I decided to include it at the end as an extra scene. If you'd like to stay in touch with me and be the first to learn about new releases, check out my website. https://www.katiereus.com

ACKNOWLEDGMENTS

I never know where to start, so in no particular order I owe thanks to Kari, Sarah, Jaycee, Kelli and Julia. You all played a different part in helping this story become an actual book. So thank you from the bottom of my heart. To my wonderful, wonderful readers, thank you for joining me on this wild ride that is the Redemption Harbor series! For my family (always), I'm grateful for your support. And of course, I'm grateful to God for so many opportunities.

COMPLETE BOOKLIST

Red Stone Security Series
No One to Trust
Danger Next Door
Fatal Deception
Miami, Mistletoe & Murder
His to Protect
Breaking Her Rules
Protecting His Witness
Sinful Seduction
Under His Protection
Deadly Fallout
Sworn to Protect
Secret Obsession
Love Thy Enemy
Dangerous Protector
Lethal Game

Redemption Harbor Series
Resurrection
Savage Rising
Dangerous Witness
Innocent Target
Hunting Danger
Covert Games
Chasing Vengeance

Sin City Series (the Serafina)
First Surrender
Sensual Surrender
Sweetest Surrender
Dangerous Surrender

Deadly Ops Series
Targeted
Bound to Danger
Chasing Danger (novella)
Shattered Duty
Edge of Danger
A Covert Affair

O'Connor Family Series
Merry Christmas, Baby
Tease Me, Baby
It's Me Again, Baby
Mistletoe Me, Baby

Non-series Romantic Suspense
Running From the Past
Dangerous Secrets
Killer Secrets
Deadly Obsession
Danger in Paradise
His Secret Past
Retribution
Tempting Danger

Paranormal Romance
Destined Mate
Protector's Mate
A Jaguar's Kiss
Tempting the Jaguar
Enemy Mine
Heart of the Jaguar

Moon Shifter Series
Alpha Instinct
Lover's Instinct
Primal Possession
Mating Instinct
His Untamed Desire
Avenger's Heat
Hunter Reborn
Protective Instinct
Dark Protector
A Mate for Christmas

Darkness Series
Darkness Awakened
Taste of Darkness
Beyond the Darkness
Hunted by Darkness
Into the Darkness
Saved by Darkness
Guardian of Darkness
Sentinel of Darkness
A Very Dragon Christmas
Darkness Rising

ABOUT THE AUTHOR

Katie Reus is the *New York Times* and *USA Today* bestselling author of the Red Stone Security series, the Darkness series and the Deadly Ops series. She fell in love with romance at a young age thanks to books she pilfered from her mom's stash. Years later she loves reading romance almost as much as she loves writing it.

However, she didn't always know she wanted to be a writer. After changing majors many times, she finally graduated summa cum laude with a degree in psychology. Not long after that she discovered a new love. Writing. She now spends her days writing dark paranormal romance and sexy romantic suspense.

For more information on Katie please visit her website: www.katiereus.com. Also find her on twitter @katiereus or visit her on facebook at: www.facebook.com/katiereusauthor.

Made in the USA
Columbia, SC
16 January 2019